Mother be the Judge

Copyright © 2014 Sally O'Brien

Mother be the Judge

SALLY O'BRIEN

For the four most important people in my life; Paul, Molly, Stanley and Max
I will love you forever x

Acknowledgements

I would like to say thank you to my friends Lisa Waterston and Lizzie Hawkes for being so supportive whilst I was writing this book and for giving me honest opinions on how I was doing. I would also like to thank Jack Frost for helping me make my dreams a reality and to the Metropolitan Police where I worked for seventeen years; without that experience I would never have known what a truly twisted world we live in.

And a big thank you to Emma Lynch, friends forever whatever the weather.

Table of Contents

Prologue

The rat picked its way through the detritus which had been caught in the reeds on the stream's edge. Its nose moved constantly, searching for a smell which would lead it to a meal. As the landscape changed from vegetation to a dark cement tunnel, the sound of cars speeding on the road overhead became more apparent. The familiar sound in this urban jungle did not deter the rat from its scavenging.

A strong meaty smell filled the rat's senses as it came across the girl's body lying slumped in the stream. Water washed over her, collecting blood from a jagged wound as it flowed over her naked chest, the small budded nipples showing the very beginnings of womanhood.

A promise of food pushed all fear of the human predator from the rat's mind and it boldly climbed the fleshy mound before it, seeking the smell that tempted its nose. When it found the ragged skin, it began to tear away the tasty morsels, eating with relish its unusual find. The girl did not flinch at the rat's bite. Her head, twisted away from her chest, half open dead eyes staring into a void unknown, mouth open but no longer able to utter a sound.

Once the rat had sated its hunger, it continued its journey along the tunnel and out once again into the heavy vegetation along the stream's bank. Fat raindrops began to fall from the sky, every drop in the stream a second of time that passed with the abandoned body awaiting discovery; another rat already answering the call of her torn flesh.

Book 1

Jocasta

Chapter 1

Jocasta - 15 years old.

"Children should be seen and not heard Jocasta. Remember we are opening our home to you, nobody else wanted you and we have been kind enough to take you in."

"Yes Charlie." Jocasta responded; eyes cast down to the floor, chewing on her lip in a bid to stop herself crying.

"Now please go up to your room and only come down when we ask you to."

"Yes Charlie, thank you." Jocasta said and walked slowly up the worn stairs, trying hard to ensure her footsteps did not cause any noise on the wooden boards. She walked into her allocated bedroom - a little box room just big enough to fit a small bed and a chest of drawers - sat on the bed which would be hers until this set of foster parents got sick of her and began to wait the eternal wait for dinner.

In her eyes, Jocasta Brown was boring, a nobody, someone to be ignored.

She had been handed over to the Social Services in the town of Olinsbury by her mother Larissa as a baby. Jocasta had been told by her Social Worker that her mother had been raped and she was the result of the brutal coupling, finally born into the world on the 1st April 1963. Being a Greek Orthodox Catholic and a very religious woman, her mother had felt unable to abort the baby so callously planted by her aggressor but Larissa also felt she was unable to live every day looking at the face of her rapist.

Since that time Jocasta had been moved constantly between foster homes. She had never suffered abuse, either physically or sexually; she had been an ideal foster child, always seen but not heard as had been drummed into her by every foster parent she had experienced. Jocasta had never rebelled or run away, she was just ignored; fed and watered like a cow on a farm and then moved on. Jocasta knew that as she was nearing 17 it would soon be time for her to be pushed out into the world, expected to fend for herself and truly alone at last. This didn't bother her, she sometimes felt the most lonely when people were around her; at least when she was by herself she could speak out loud and give herself an answer. At least when she was alone she could dream that her life was ok. Just ok, she didn't need it to be brilliant, exciting or challenging, ok would do, she would love for her life to just be ok.

* * *

Mother Be The Judge

Jocasta - 17 years old.

Jocasta was given the keys to a two bedroomed flat on a council estate known as Fern Bridge. It was in the Olinsbury borough of Elisworth, West London; an unremarkable borough with its only claim to fame being a one-time residence of an artist with a name Jocasta could not pronounce.

The social worker dropped Jocasta at the front door of her new flat and wished her well. Jocasta turned the key in the grey front door and walked into her new life. The flat had been sparsely furnished by the Youth Help Team and Jocasta surveyed her unmade bed in the first room she came across. She wondered how she would be able to afford bed linen with the paltry sum of money she had been allocated but was still excited at the prospect of being able to put *her* clean sheets on *her* own bed. Taking a pen and paper from her handbag, Jocasta sat on the floor of her new home and began to make a list of necessary items to make her existence bearable. Biscuits were top of the list, everything was ok as long as she had a biscuit in her hand and there was no one around now to tell her when to stop eating them, maybe her life was going to be ok after all, she thought.

* * *

Jocasta continued to live her adult life as she had

lived her childhood; no dramas, no love affairs. A nice safe job as a doctor's receptionist kept her busy and ensured she was able to furnish her flat. She had slowly built the contents of her home, adding a new item each time she got paid and was happy there. Although her home and job were sorted, Jocasta knew that she was still a boring nobody; no one in the surgery ever spoke to her unless it was regarding work. They didn't know if she was single or married, happy or sad; didn't even know that Bourbons were her favourite biscuit. She just carried on in life, eyes down, lip chewed, ignored by one and all.

The only interesting thing about Jocasta was her name, but as she had no idea where it came from, that was guaranteed to stop any conversation before it started.

Chapter 2

Shirley Valentine, "That's right Millandra; I'm going to Greece for the sex. Sex for breakfast, sex for dinner, sex for tea and sex for supper."

Van Driver, "Sounds like a fantastic diet love."

Shirley Valentine, "It is, have you never heard of it? It's called the F plan."

Author Unknown.

December 1989

The bump of the plane touching the runway caused Jocasta Brown to release the breath she had unconsciously been holding onto since the plane began to descend. It marked the end to a whirlwind month for Jocasta after she had made the first spontaneous decision of her twenty six year life to emulate Shirley Valentine and seek a new chapter in Mykonos, Greece.

* * *

Going to see the film, on her own as usual, inspired her; Jocasta realised she wasn't the only woman in the world who felt ignored and unloved. Worrying she would never feel the love of a man either emotionally or physically she made a decision in the cinema that she would finally take some time off from her drab job as a doctor's receptionist; she knew her roots were in Greece and she believed that fate had led her to the film and would also lead her to the Travel Agents. It was time to get herself a Costas, just like Shirley.

Three days, a long wait at the passport office - well it's not like she had ever needed a passport before - a manic shop for suitcase, clothes and hair remover and Jocasta was ready to take her flight.

Jocasta entered the airport for the first time in her life. She couldn't open her eyes wide enough to take in her surroundings. She felt a rush of nausea as she started to feel there was no way she would be able to work out where the check-in desk was; the queues of people just seemed to go on and on, luggage littered on the floor in front of confused looking groups of people. Children either screaming or hysterically laughing causing their parents to fidget in agitation whilst they waited their turn to check-in. Jocasta took out her paperwork once again and began to go through it, hoping it would give some clue as to which desk she needed to be at.

After thoroughly reading every word on her flight itinerary, Jocasta could only make the decision to find a sign which gave the name of the company she was flying with. She walked along the concourse, eyes flitting left and right hoping to see the sign she wanted; finally as she neared the end and was starting to believe she may be in the wrong terminal, she saw

Mother Be The Judge

the dull light from a board announcing 'Greek Air, Check-In'. Thankful that she hadn't given up looking as her feet were already aching just from the walk to find her check-in point, Jocasta took her place in a queue of people who looked either bored or severely pissed off. She was neither of these things and couldn't imagine why people would feel this way when they were off on their holidays.

Twenty minutes later and even Jocasta's enthusiasm for her journey could not stop her face from mirroring that of the other people in her queue. The wait seemed interminable; every passenger in front of her had a problem and where she had originally been amused at seeing cases opened and clothes being flung out, knickers and all, while people tried to decide what they should leave behind; Jocasta was now starting to contemplate her own fate when she finally reached the check-in point.

Two hours later, yet another queue to actually get on the plane and Jocasta found herself struggling to fit into the airplane's seat. The belt which was on her chair just would not fit across her legs; she attempted to hide the fact it was undone when the flight attendant came to check but he took great pleasure in announcing loudly to his co-attendee that they would require an extension for seat 34. Jocasta didn't bother to thank him as he reached over to hand her the belt; she could see his amusement was thanks enough. Lowering her eyes to avoid eye contact with the people sitting beside her, Jocasta concentrated on thinking about leaving the ground. It seemed wrong somehow that a tin can with rigid wings would be shooting up into the air and flying her at five hundred miles an hour over land and sea. The pathetic piece of fabric which was her belt, even with its extension could not possibly aid her in an emergency where the plane was crashing into the sea below. Jocasta felt her palms sweating and her heart pounding at the prospect of leaving terra firma, however, she was so excited at the prospect of being the next Shirley Valentine and confident that she would discover herself in Greece that as the plane took off her nerves dissipated and she actually began to enjoy the flight. Apart from the occasional bump it was no different to being on a very large bus and Jocasta made good use of the 'trolley dollies' or the 'arseholes' as she was now want to secretly call them, who offered her fancy packets of peanuts and pretzels with every Diet Coke she purchased and her own stash of biscuits made sure she didn't go hungry on the seven hour flight.

On reaching her affordable hotel, she found it was basic and functional although she didn't want to chance cooking anything on the antiquated cooker in her self-catered apartment. Jocasta made use of her hair removal cream, removing the shrubbery around her pubic area, ridding her armpits of their bristly companions and parting her one eyebrow into two. She gave her teeth a thorough clean and floss rather than her usual cursory brushing and then put on her new blue summer dress. Jocasta assessed herself in the small bathroom mirror; her eyebrows now had far too big a gap between them and had taken on a life of their own; one apparently happy to be above her eye while the other looking as though it wanted to be elsewhere. She decided she may leave eyebrow shaping to the professionals in future. Her brown eyes stared back at her with a shiny hint of excitement in them instead of their usual bored look. She was well covered by her dress; hiding her bulky undefined body underneath. Jocasta felt she looked nice and was ready to face her new life as a single woman looking for love.

Jocasta spent the first few days exploring the island; unhappily hot with constant sweat streaming from every pore of her body. Her Greek roots did her no favours as every drenched item of her clothing reminded her. She had tried to sunbathe and do the 'tourist' thing but the heat was too much to bear and sunbathing was quite possibly the most boring thing Jocasta had ever done. She resolved to keep out of the sun as much as possible and decided to stick to air conditioned restaurants or shaded areas in taverna gardens, where she could read her newly acquired stockpile of books. Her initial anticipation of a new chapter in her life had been quelled by the sweat which continued to drench her even when in shade.

On the fourth day of Jocasta's trip she ventured into a taverna called Dimitri's. Stepping into the leafy shade of the garden offered her some relief from the sun. She sat at a table with the blue and white striped linen which seemed to adorn every table in Mykonos. The bright blue chairs against the white washed walls and the scent from the olive trees made her feel content and she smiled happily at the barman as he took her order for a jug of lemonade then settled down to read her book. The barman there was very kind to Jocasta and visited her table often to replenish her drink and to offer her humus and pitta bread along with some very fat olives. He was not a conventionally handsome man, he had dark curly hair and piercing blue eyes which stared out of a leathery face, that at one time had been ravaged by acne; deep scars bearing testament to the teenage affliction. His teeth were yellowed and uneven, one top tooth sticking out slightly whenever he smiled at her. He smelled heavily of garlic and sweat but rather than being turned off by it, Jocasta found the heady smell very manly and attractive.

"Yassou," he greeted her. Jocasta had no idea what he meant; was he offering her food?

"Sorry, I don't speak Greek." She told him. He chuckled and then said, "It means 'hello'"

"Oh," Jocasta wondered why he had said that, he had already spoken to her earlier to take her order, he knew she was English. "Yassou, to you as well," she offered.

"What is your name pretty lady?" he came to sit beside her. Jocasta's heart gave a little jump, had he just called her pretty?

"Jocasta," she replied.

"Ah Jocasta, the mother of Oedipus," he nodded, "Are you Greek?"

"My mother was, but this is my first time here." Jocasta said. "Who is Oedipus?"

He gave another chuckle and said, "Just a person from Greek Mythology. You have lovely eyes. My name is Avram. Avram Dimitriades"

"Like Costas." Jocasta gasped.

"Who is Costas?" Avram smiled

"Oh no one, it's from a film I've been watching." Jocasta blushed as she realised Avram was staring intently at her.

"Ah the Shirley Valentine yes?" Laughed Avram, "We have been getting lots of them here." He got up from beside her and tapped the table with his finger. "Maybe I make you *my* Shirley yes?" he smiled and returned to his place behind the bar.

After Jocasta had remained in her chair for the afternoon, reading, drinking her lemonade and then ordering a dinner of Keftedes; a meal of beef and lamb meatballs which Avram had assured her were delicious, she paid her bill and made to leave.

"You will come back tomorrow yes Shirley?" Avram asked her. "We can have dinner together yes?"

"Yes." Jocasta replied too quickly and almost with a shout. She blushed once again then left the taverna, looking over her shoulder at Avram who smiled and waved as she walked away.

Jocasta felt sure the fact Avram shared the same surname as Shirley's beau was fated and this liaison was meant to be; on this holiday her life was going to be more than ok, she just knew it.

* * *

Avram introduced her to the sights of Greece and took her shopping, although it was Jocasta's purse which always seemed to provide the money; Avram was a low paid waiter whereas she had a rather substantial fund of savings which she had never had cause to spend whilst in her home town and boring life. Avram swept Jocasta away on a constant stream of attention, she was overwhelmed by the friendship he bestowed on her and she found herself laughing and conversing like an ordinary person; listened to and laughed with, her company seemingly enjoyed. Avram would wink at her as he worked and give her free drinks then take her for walks along the beach in the cooler evenings; hand in hand, chatting about his desire to visit England and see where Jocasta lived.

Into the third week of Jocasta's month long holiday and Avram took Jocasta to a beach called Agios Ioannis after work. The sun was setting as they sat on the pebbled and sandy beach, Avram pointed out the island of Delos in the distance and explained that the beach they were on was the beach where Shirley Valentine had been filmed and it was one of the places in the world where the sun is brighter than anywhere else.

"Just like my love for you." He said, "Brighter than the love I have ever felt for anyone else."

Jocasta's breath caught in her throat. When he had looked deep into her eyes and uttered the words Jocasta had never hoped to hear, she was overcome with emotion and cried tears of joy.

"Hey Jocasta, don't cry," Avram said, taking her in

Mother Be The Judge

his arms. He began to kiss her and they lay in the sand for a long time kissing and touching each other until the sun went down. As the darkness came upon them Avram became more passionate in his kissing and began to pull at Jocasta's skirt. Jocasta knew this was probably the moment when her virginity was going to be taken and she pulled out of Avram's embrace when a strong fear arose in her.

"What's the matter Jocasta, don't you want to?" Avram asked disappointedly. "It's time, yes? Come on."

"I," Jocasta didn't know how to tell Avram that she was a virgin. "I've never done this before." She breathed. Avram gave a low chuckle.

"Well I have," he assured her. "Don't you worry Shirley, leave it all to me." He said then began to reach for her once more.

Jocasta realised this was her make or break decision. If she walked away now she would probably never see Avram again.

"But... what if I'm not good at.... it?" she asked him to more laughter.

"Jocasta, you don't need to be good at anything, that's my job." They began to kiss once again and she allowed herself to go with whatever Avram wanted. He pulled her skirt and underwear away from her and began to touch her labia, pushing at them with his fingers to reach her vagina underneath. Jocasta could only wonder at whether she had done a good enough job with her bikini line and whether Avram would think she was too hairy or her vagina was the wrong shape or size. She was grateful it was dark and she couldn't see his face; or him hers. Suddenly Avram pulled away from her and began to pull Jocasta up off the sand.

"What's the matter?" she asked him, 'there's something wrong with me'; she thought.

"Nothing," his voice was lower and more gravelly, "I just like it this way." He told her. He placed her on her hands and knees and pushed her head down towards the sand. She was almost taking in a mouthful of sand when she felt a sharp pain in her vagina. Jocasta bit her finger so as not to call out as she didn't want Avram to know that he had hurt her. He continued to pound into her, knocking her head into the sand until finally he gave a loud sigh and stopped. Avram moved away from Jocasta leaving her in the sand with her arse up in the air. She didn't know if she was expected to move so just stayed in that position as Avram began to get dressed. He looked at her in amusement.

"You can get up now Jocasta." He said. She pushed herself onto her knees and took the skirt and underwear from the sand beside her then got dressed.

"How was that?" Avram asked

"Amazing," Jocasta said. She wanted to please Avram and didn't think her real answer of "Unexpected and painful," would make him feel good about his sexual prowess. Having learnt what sex was all about Jocasta was pleased that she didn't have any chance of a repeat performance when she got back to England. If that was what love was about, they could keep it.

"Come on, I have to go." Avram said, he got up

from the sand and began to walk away, ignoring the hand Jocasta had offered for help from the ground. She followed him quietly, feeling a growing sense that Avram maybe didn't like her as much as he had been professing over the last few days.

"Avram," she called after him.

"Yes my darling?" Avram called back without looking.

"What's the matter, was I ok?" she asked.

"Yes, fine." He replied then turned back to wait for her. "Listen I have to work tomorrow but you can come to the restaurant, we can go shopping in my break yes?"

"Shopping?" she asked him, Jocasta couldn't think of anything else Avram could possibly want; she had already spent so much money on him.

"Yes, I really need some new shoes." He said, "Maybe I buy something nice for you, yes?" he reached out to stroke her hair then gently planted a kiss on her face. Jocasta found herself blushing, to kiss her like that he *must* love her, she was just being silly thinking she was being used.

"Yes ok Avram, I will see you tomorrow. How are we getting back?" she wondered.

"Oh I have to go and see some family in the hills so I can't go back with you, but you can get a taxi from over there." Avram pointed out a line of cars on the road in the distance.

"Sorry Jocasta but I really have to go." He said then kissed her once more before walking quickly away.

Jocasta walked towards the taxi rank, once more alone but she had a hot feeling in her vagina where Avram had been and it throbbed as she walked. It may not have been the way she had read it in books - rolling on a sea of hot emotion, climaxing together, transported into a world of love - but it had still happened; she was no longer a virgin, *somebody* loved her and that was good enough for her.

* * *

Avram had introduced Jocasta to a sex life where she accepted roughness as passion and friendship as foreplay. She decided the clitoris was a thing of fiction as it never did anything for her and Avram paid it no attention; he took her whenever or wherever the feeling came over him, often from behind and in silence. Jocasta was so enamoured by Avram that she acquiesced to his sexual urges, but knew sex was not something she would miss when she returned home.

The month went by so fast and she had loved every day. As the third week ended and the fourth week began, Avram had cooled in his affections towards her. Jocasta's now dwindling pot of money prevented them from shopping and she was no longer able to bestow gifts of clothes and aftershave upon him. She had nothing more to offer Avram other than herself and she could see he had shifted his focus onto new arrivals to the restaurant, rather than on soon to be departed Jocasta.

It hadn't mattered; it was only ever going to be her one wild moment of her life. Jocasta was pleased her holiday had brought her love, even if it was momentary; she was happy to return to her boring safe life and was looking forward to returning to her work. Jocasta wondered if the other girls who worked in the surgery would notice her glow or suspect the loss of her virginity; she knew that was highly unlikely as they would probably continue to ignore her. She consoled herself with the fact that *she* would know and would always have her memories of Avram even if she had no one to share those memories with.

* * *

The seatbelt signs went off and Jocasta stood up to collect her overhead baggage, only to find herself stumble as she was overcome by dizziness and nausea. She hoped she hadn't caught a bug; that was *not* the memory she wanted to end this holiday of a lifetime on.

Chapter 3

'The moment a child is born the mother is also born. She never existed before. The woman existed but the mother, never. A mother is something absolutely new.'

Rajneesh

19 August 1990

"Ok, I can see the head; just one more push when I say."

The midwife looked up at Jocasta who was silently praying that this final push was actually the one which was going to bring her little boy out into the world. What a nine months it had been; after realising that the 'bug' she had picked up in Greece was going on for a bit too long and that her period had never come on its allocated date, Jocasta was shocked but delighted to find that she was pregnant.

Although it had never been her intention to bring back this kind of souvenir, actually Jocasta realised that this was what she had been longing for all her life. A little person of her own, a family member; someone who would love her as much as she wanted to be loved and someone whom she could love back.

The next nine months were a time of wonder and

amazement, reading books about how the little fellow was growing. Parenting manuals, ante-natal classes, yoga, shopping and decorating the nursery in her two bedroomed flat consumed her time. Jocasta had never been so busy. She went from being a bored, lonely workaholic into a busy workaholic who was soon to never be lonely again.

Watching her body changing was astounding. Every day Jocasta looked at herself in the mirror. She was nothing to look at; she knew that; mousy brown hair always in a ponytail pulled severely off her face. Dark brown eyes under hooded eyebrows which were tirelessly fighting to become one, full nose and thin lips and quite a thick chin, even Jocasta didn't find herself attractive. Her body was much the same as her face; hairy and thick, small where it shouldn't be and large everywhere else. As the months went on her body blossomed, breasts grew and the largeness of her stomach now seemed right as there was a reason for the ever present bump.

"Aaaah, please, please let this be the one." Her fanny actually felt as if it was being pushed off of her body, she wanted to reach down and hold onto it to stop it falling off. "Please, is he coming?"

"Yes, yes, don't worry, his head is coming out, just pant a little bit for me Jocasta, there's a good girl."

"Pant, what do you mean pant?" The notion seemed ridiculous to Jocasta, even though she had heard it in the ante-natal classes the reality of the situation didn't come close and panting was the last thing on this earth that she felt she could do.

"Just little shallow breaths, we don't want him to come out too fast, you're doing really well Jocasta, keep it up."

Well it's not like she could actually stop doing what she was doing was it? This whole scenario seemed as though it was happening to somebody else and Jocasta suddenly found it hilarious bursting out into uncontrolled laughter.

"That's great panting, keep it up," the midwife stated, "Here he comes, one final push."

Suddenly just when Jocasta thought that she was going to be the first woman ever to explode giving birth, there was an immense feeling of release from her vagina, a tidal wave of water and body parts landed on the bed in front of her and then a little mew of sound from her son. Her son, he was here.

The midwife quickly grabbed the baby and put him onto Jocasta's belly, he felt hot and slippery and looked like he had just been daubed in a tub of grease but oh my, here he was, Adrian, a name she found in a book of Greek boys' names and instantly fell in love with.

"Congratulations, he's lovely," smiled the midwife.

"Thank you, yes he is lovely. Thank you."

Adrian was taken away whilst Jocasta was washed and stitched, then helped to sit up so she could give him his first feed. Suddenly there was the sound of a panic alarm and what Jocasta thought must be a doctor ran into the room; going straight to Adrian. Jocasta realised there must be a problem. She felt a large lump rise in her throat and the urge to scream overtook her,

"What's wrong?" she cried, "What's wrong?"

Once again in her life she was being ignored, all eyes were on the small baby lying in the cot. She couldn't see if his chest was rising, he was very quiet but still a nice colour she thought. He couldn't be dead could he? Why wouldn't anyone tell her what was going on? She heard Adrian give a little cry again which appeased her worrying, she knew that he was alive at least, but she didn't think it was normal for a baby to need so much attention from doctors when it was born.

"Please tell me, what the matter is?" she asked once again.

"Your baby has a strangulated testicle," the doctor said to her. "It's causing a problem in his groin area and we need to act fast to stop the problem. Don't worry, once he has had a small operation he will be absolutely fine. We just need your consent to take him away and get it sorted."

A clipboard was shoved under her face and Jocasta signed it without reading it; she wouldn't have been able to take it all in as she was so worried.

"Please make him ok." She said.

"Don't worry, it's a very quick operation, he will be fine."

* * *

Jocasta was so tired from her long labour that even the worry of Adrian's operation couldn't stop her body from shutting down. She lay back, closed her eyes and instantaneously fell asleep. She was awoken by the midwife just an hour later and Jocasta found Adrian was back at her bedside in his plastic crib, dressed in one of the yellow baby grows she had bought him. He wasn't ready to feed yet as they still needed to monitor him after the anaesthetic; she had expressed milk for him which she was asked to put down a tube in his nose. It didn't feel right that she should just be holding a syringe in the air and watching milk flow down a tube into a baby, how was she meant to bond with a syringe?

It was hard for Jocasta to now feel like a mother. She was sore, tired, shocked and worried about Adrian. No book or class had prepared her for this feeling of emptiness now that Adrian had left her womb; she missed his presence there and couldn't equate the bump with the baby. What was she supposed to do now? Who was going to come and tell her how to look after Adrian? When was he supposed to be fed? How did she actually change a nappy when there was a living breathing soul inside it? What if he didn't like her? What if he saw her as the boring, ugly, ignorable person that everyone else in this world seemed to? What had she done? This was not the picture Jocasta had put in her mind for the time after the birth. She had visualised sitting on the hospital bed cooing over her bundle of joy swaddled in his blue blanket and him smiling - wind - up at her. She was going to take him home and put him in his crib and then they would live happily ever after. It was shocking to Jocasta that the reality was a sick baby, an extremely battered body and an overwhelming sense of fear.

* * *

After spending the next two hours waiting for a nurse, midwife, anyone, to come and take Adrian away or tell her what to do with him; Adrian woke up. He made an almost catlike sound and then his little arms began to stretch out whilst his head went back. Jocasta peered into the crib and saw Adrian's eyes for the first time, they were very dark, colourless, shiny orbs, moving independently of each other; Jocasta thought they were the most beautiful eyes she had ever seen. She reached in and picked him up as she couldn't wait any longer for somebody to tell her what to do. Instinctively bringing him into her body she looked down onto this child she had waited for, for so long. Love engulfed her; she could actually feel its warming presence begin somewhere at the top of her head and start to envelope her. Jocasta opened her eyes as wide as she could so she could drink in the very sight of this child, her child, her son. She couldn't say that he would be beautiful to others, in fact he was downright ugly in a baby sort of way; but he was hers and to her he was precious and beautiful. There was no one else anywhere in the universe that had an interest in looking after this child, no one who would love him like she could, no one who would show him the world and all its delights. Jocasta realised that this was the bond everyone speaks about. It had taken so long to happen that Jocasta was starting to question herself, but now here it was in full force. She never wanted to put Adrian down, never wanted to lose the warmth and the heaviness of his body. He was here, she had done it and she was a mother.

Mother Be The Judge

Chapter 4

'There is only one pretty child in the world and every mother has it.'

Chinese proverb

5 September 1994

"Adrian it's time to get up; come on." Jocasta stopped dead as she entered Arian's bedroom. He was already out of bed and was studying what looked like the remains of a dead kitten on his bed.

"Adrian, what *are* you doing with that?" she asked him, rushing over to his bed to pull him away from it. The kitten had blood coming from around its mouth and one of its eyes was now lying on the bed, still attached by its vein to the socket. Jocasta held her mouth and tried to avert her eyes so she wouldn't be sick at the sight of it.

"I found it mummy." Adrian told her and reached out for the kitten, she pulled him further back and took him out of the bedroom into the kitchen where she could find a black bag to put the kitten in.

"Where did you find it?" she asked him; Adrian was only four years old and restricted to the outside communal landing for playtime, she couldn't imagine where he could have found a dead cat out there.

"It was in the landing so I brought it in." Adrian told her.

"You found a dead cat outside?" she asked.

"Well he wasn't dead when I found him." Adrian said looking at the floor. Jocasta was confused, how did he find a live kitten in the hallway and then somehow it became dead in his bedroom with its eye hanging out.

"Well what happened Adrian?" she asked, "How did the cat die?"

Adrian did not reply, instead choosing to look at the floor. He would not lift his head and look at Jocasta, she realised he must have done something wrong. Jocasta got onto her knees so that their faces were level and took his chin in her hand, lifting his face so that he had to make eye contact with her; even in these shocking circumstances she couldn't help but feel her heart melt as she looked into his beautiful eyes.

"Adrian, mummy is not going to be cross but you need to tell me what happened ok?"

Adrian started to sob, "I'm sorry mummy, I didn't mean it; I just wanted to play with it."

He reached out his arms for her and her heart melted even more; she took him into her embrace and held him for a short while. Jocasta believed that Adrian must have had an accident with the kitten whilst he was trying to play. It was her fault for never having introduced him to animals before and showing him how to be gentle with them. Jocasta chided herself for not being a better parent. She brought Adrian out of her embrace to face him again.

"Look Adrian, it doesn't matter, it was a mistake. But you mustn't bring animals into the house ok?"

"Yes mummy."

"And you must always be gentle with them ok?"

"Yes mummy."

"Now how about I take you to the farm on Saturday?" Jocasta asked. Adrian's face lit up and he said, "Yeah."

"Ok now go to the bathroom and brush your teeth, it's your first day at school today and we don't want to be late."

"Ok mummy." Adrian said and skipped off to the bathroom. Jocasta retrieved a black bag from under the kitchen sink and went back into the bedroom to dispose of the kitten. On closer inspection the kitten's neck looked far too long for its body as it if had been stretched. How the eye had come out of its socket was a mystery to Jocasta but she supposed that Adrian must have cuddled the cat just a little bit too tightly and suffocated it. Jocasta hoped that this episode would not have a detrimental effect on Adrian; she felt terrible for him and worried that he may have nightmares about the poor kitten. She knew now that she couldn't allow Adrian to play outside of the flat away from her again, even on the landing; it just caused too many problems. Jocasta decided the best thing to do would be to pretend it had never happened, Adrian would have forgotten all about it by the time he came home from school; she was more worried how he would cope with a day away from her.

Jocasta put the kitten in with the household rubbish and when they left for school she went to the rubbish chute and tipped the bag inside. She heard the next door neighbour calling, "Here kitty, kitty." And realised that he must have purchased the kitten recently; holding down her guilt and determined to keep her mouth shut about the whole episode, Jocasta grasped Adrian's hand and they began to make their journey to his new school.

* * *

Jocasta's heart felt very heavy as she stood in Elisworth Town School's playground. This was Adrian's first day at school, first day ever of being away from his mother and first day really of the rest of his life.

After having Adrian, Jocasta's plans to return to work were scuppered by her inability to leave the child alone. He consumed her very being and was her reason for waking up each morning. Where work had been her only companion, Adrian had taken over any wants that Jocasta had.

She didn't need anything else in her life, indeed for the first week she had actually forgotten to eat anything. It was only when the health visitor came for her final visit to sign Jocasta and Adrian off as fit, that the health visitor noted Jocasta's pallor and asked her if she had been eating. The realisation that if she didn't eat and keep herself well then her baby would suffer too, spurred Jocasta into taking better care of herself.

Since then she had done nothing but what was right for Adrian and made sure that she was fit and healthy enough to look after him; a happy coincidence of this was that Jocasta now had the figure of a woman instead of a lumpy potato. Not that anyone noticed; it hadn't changed her invisibility where every other human on this planet was concerned.

* * *

As Jocasta stood in the playground she took in her surroundings. The grounds were that of a typical primary school with tricycles and hula hoops dotted about on the rubber coated tarmac. There were mums and dads standing with their children, all waiting for the start of their first day at school. It was obvious to Jocasta that a lot of the parents were familiar with each other as they were chatting amiably together, comfortable in each other's company. She could hear snippets of conversation where they all talked about how their summers had been, children largely ignored as they hung off their parents or ran around with each other. It was also sadly obvious to Jocasta that *she* was the subject of many conversations.

"Look at the state of her." One dark haired woman said to her anorexic friend. The friend nodded and added, "Fuck her, it's the kid; look at it, hit every branch of the ugly tree that one."

"Yeah," laughed the dark haired woman, "When

he was born the doctor gave *her* a slap." Both fell about laughing, before moving onto their next victim. Jocasta took a deep breath and stroked Adrian's head. He seemed oblivious to their comments so she decided not to take it any further.

She knew that Adrian was unlike the other children. He was still beautiful to her but he was unlike the other cute and angelic children who played so care free around her. Unfortunately he had taken on the worst parts of both Jocasta and Avram alike; he had dark bristly hair which stood in unruly curls. A very thick monobrow which sat over hooded dirty blue eyes and one of his top teeth stuck out in the same peculiar way as his father's had. He was also extremely skinny, which made his feet seem much larger than they were. Jocasta looked down on him and stroked his hair, a lump forming in her throat at the thought of having to leave him at the classroom door.

A loud alarm signalled the start of the school day and the classroom doors opened. All the children were encouraged by the teacher to form a line outside the classroom door. Adrian had been standing silently beside his mother until this moment, unsure of where he was and what was going to happen. Jocasta *had* told him about school and that he was going to meet new friends and learn about the world. She manoeuvred him into the line and stood back in the throng of parents surrounding the line of children.

A piercing scream cut through the melee of jostling school children. Two small hands reached for Jocasta's trouser leg and she looked down to find the

Mother Be The Judge

scream was coming from Adrian. Fat tears streamed from his eyes, "Mummy no." he cried, "No, I don't want to go, mummy don't leave me." The scream turned into a cry with much gasping for air, causing Adrian's head to jerk back in an alarming manner. Snot streamed from his nose and Jocasta had never felt more helpless.

She had put this off for a year already, choosing not to send Adrian to nursery as it wasn't the law and she wanted to keep him to herself for another year. It had not occurred to her that to send him to nursery was to gently break him into the routine of school life and would help him fit in at 'big school'. No, Jocasta was not going to give up her time with her son that easily, she could not and would not cut any cords with Adrian until she had to, he was hers and she was going to keep him to herself for as long as she possibly could.

"Just leave him with me, he will be fine." A large hand appeared on Adrian's shoulder; Jocasta looked up to see a male who was looking at her with a sympathetic expression on his face. He was dressed all in brown, comfortable clothing which had never seen an iron. He had brown scruffy hair which looked as if he ran his hands through it constantly. The male did that now as he addressed Jocasta, "I'm Mr Martin, his teacher, don't worry it is always hard for them at first but by Christmas they are all skipping in quite happily."

"I can't just leave him here when he's being like this, he needs me." Jocasta's attempt to take control of the situation was falling on deaf ears.

"No it's fine; there are always a couple of kids who can't cope at first." He gestured towards the door where another young boy was holding on to his mother's skirt whilst she was pushing him gently through the door into the arms of the waiting teacher.

"Honestly, he will be fine. If you want, you can call us in an hour and we will let you know how he's getting on. The number is on his entry letter." Mr Martin took hold of Adrian and gently unclenched Adrian's fists from Jocasta's trousers.

Jocasta didn't know what she could do to help Adrian. It felt as though she was throwing him to the wolves, not taking him to school. She just wanted to pick him up and run away from this place as fast as she possibly could and it was all she could do not to go with her instincts. Feeling emotion bubbling up inside her Jocasta turned away from Adrian and Mr Martin and walked stiffly to the school gates, Adrian's cries echoing in her ears. She could not look back as she knew to see his anguished face again would make her act on her emotions.

With a choking cry she set off for home, ignoring the looks she got from other mothers and trying not to listen to the barely concealed whispers.

"What an ugly child, did you see all that snot; disgusting."

"His mother's no better, hairy witch"

"Fucking weirdos if you ask me."

"There's always one nutter wherever you go."

"Yeah well I'm telling my Billy to keep away from him."

Biting down on her urge to shout at the parents to fuck right off, Jocasta turned and left the playground, the insults ringing in her ears.

Mother Be The Judge

The last four years of Jocasta and Adrian's lives had been safe, innocuous, protected and joyful. Just the two of them together, loving each other and enjoying each other's company. Their world was now being torn apart for the sake of education. Jocasta felt as though Adrian had been ripped from her arms and cast into a world which was callous and unforgiving. They wouldn't understand what a wonderful child he was, they wouldn't see him as she did. All they would see was his face, which to them was ugly and didn't conform to their idea of perfect. To her he was beautiful, to them he was ugly. To her he was angelic; to them he was a daemon by virtue of his looks. Never would they look past his face to find the beauty inside, he would be tormented and challenged all his life because his face didn't fit.

"No." Jocasta shouted into the air, but continued to walk home just the same; there was nothing she could do about the law. She let herself into her flat, ran to the kitchen, grabbed a packet of chocolate biscuits and sat on the once immaculate sofa in her front room, chomping one biscuit after the other, barely tasting them in her haste to shove them down her gullet. She heard the next door neighbour in the corridor once again calling for his kitten which just made her feel even worse, for Adrian, who must surely be suffering from his terrible experience that morning. Looking at the clock she sat quietly eating and she waited until the time her beloved son could be saved from his wretched day.

Chapter 5

'One good mother is worth a hundred schoolmasters.'
Ralph Waldo Emerson

15 December 1996

Jocasta waited in the reception area of Elisworth Town Primary School. She had received a telephone call from the school secretary that morning asking her to come and visit the Head Master of the school, Mr Cross. The secretary would not divulge to Jocasta the reason for the visit, just stating that it was serious and could not wait until another day.

Jocasta had waited for the bus, her imagination running away with her as to what the reason could be for being called so promptly into school. Had Adrian been beaten up? Had he finally managed to achieve a grade in reading and she was being called in to be congratulated? She had smirked at the thought of that; even if Adrian *had* managed to conform to their standards of reading, she doubted very much that they would bother to congratulate her for it.

The school hadn't changed in the thirty years since she had attended there; the walls were still a dirty cream colour and there was still a bare green covering on the floor, too thin to be considered a carpet, but new enough that it wasn't the same one she had walked on as a child. There was a familiar smell to the school which had a calming effect on Jocasta, she had been mercilessly bullied in the playground when she had attended and she had sought sanctuary often in the reception area; protected by the school administrators who were sympathetic to her plight. Many days had been spent by Jocasta counting the stains on the carpet and drawing imaginary lines between each one, creating pictures with her mind to pass the boredom in the self-imposed prison each afternoon.

The door creaked open in front of her and a male walked out with purpose, presenting himself in front of Jocasta.

"Thank you for coming in Mrs Brown."

"It's Miss Brown."

The raised eyebrow was not lost on Jocasta; it was a standard response to her being a single parent. She never hid the fact, she was proud to be the sole owner of her little boy.

"I'm Mr Cross, headmaster of the school, please follow me." Mr Cross turned and walked back through the creaking door without looking back, obviously confident that Jocasta would follow him as instructed, she didn't know why he insisted on introducing himself to her every time they met; they had already had a few parent, teacher consultations since Adrian had started school. Jocasta followed Mr Cross down a long narrow hallway which was impossibly hot as every radiator seemed to be on full blast regardless of whether warmth had already been achieved. Jocasta glimpsed through windowed doors which were lined periodically along the corridor. She saw row upon row of children sitting at their desks, some with hands in the air obviously desperate to be the one to give the right answer. At one stage she thought she saw Adrian standing sullenly near a window, staring at the class before him; she didn't have a chance to confirm what she had seen as Mr Cross continued to stride along the corridor and she knew if she didn't keep up she could quite possibly get lost or reprimanded for her tardiness.

Finally at the end of the hallway, Mr Cross directed Jocasta into an office, it was a rectangle room covered in the felt boards which were familiar to schools, dotted with the hand drawings of pupils and with pictures of smiling school children holding aloft plaques and trophies which had been won. Jocasta sat in the chair indicated to her by Mr Cross.

"Yes sorry, *Miss* Brown, thank you for coming in to see me today, I'm afraid we need to speak about your son's behaviour." Mr Cross sat behind his standard council issue desk. He looked decidedly like his name at this point and Jocasta experienced a flutter deep in the pit of her stomach. What could a six year old boy have done to evoke such apparent anger in the head master of his school?

"Has he been disrupting the class again?" enquired Jocasta, "He has never really settled properly in school, I think he finds it difficult being away from home."

"We have discussed his settling in before Miss

Mother Be The Judge

Brown; I am still of the opinion that Adrian is suffering from attention deficit disorder..."

"That's just jargon..." Jocasta began her usual defence when faced with Adrian's problems.

"Mrs Brown." Mr Cross's sharp interruption took Jocasta by surprise. He was usually quite ready to listen to her side of the matter. "Mrs Brown, I haven't asked you here because of that although that is still a concern for me."

"Well why *am* I here then?"

"You are here because Adrian has assaulted one of his classmates."

"He's been in a fight? I'm sure he didn't start it, he..."

Mr Cross put his hand up stopping Jocasta once again from stating her case. "Not a fight Mrs Brown, please allow me to finish."

"Go on then." She didn't know what was coming but Jocasta could feel her hackles rising waiting for another ridiculous accusation levied at her son.

"Adrian took a female classmate into the boy's toilets today against her will and put his hands in her underwear."

"I'm sorry Mr Cross, he did what?" She wondered if he had actually just said, 'put his hands in her underwear' or if she had just imagined it."

"I know it must be difficult to hear but you heard right; Adrian has sexually assaulted a young girl in his class, she is very distressed and her parents..."

"Whoa, hold on there, *sexually assaulted*? He's six years old, an innocent child. How can you class anything he does as criminal? He doesn't know what he's doing, he's a baby." Jocasta's voice was rising as panic overtook her.

"Mrs Brown, please calm down." The head master came around to Jocasta's side of the desk and placed a hand on her shoulder. "It was the wrong choice of words, I'm sorry." He reassured her. "Of course we understand that Adrian is a very young boy, still learning right from wrong, but in light of Adrian's..." He paused, searching for the right word, "Problems, and what appears to be an escalation of his behaviour, we feel it necessary for you to have him assessed properly so we can move forwards and help him with his condition." Mr Cross stopped and a benevolent smile wiped its way across his face. "Now Mrs Brown, the girl's parents have been informed but I am pleased to tell you they agree it was probably just innocent play and are happy not to take this any further." He returned to his side of the desk and his decidedly higher chair, "What we need to do now is..."

Jocasta sat in stunned silence as the head master talked at her about special needs, behavioural problems and blah, blah. Was this really her boy they were talking about?

Her sweet, sunny and loving Adrian; her one and only son?

When he was at home they had such a close loving friendship with each other. Jocasta could not do enough for Adrian; she catered to his every need and desire. He never behaved badly when he was with her, how could this be the same child?

Mother Be The Judge

She decided that actually, no, once again the face didn't fit. Other children were obviously making up lies to get Adrian into trouble. Behavioural problems were just the schools excuse to get rid of their square peg. They would not win. Her Adrian deserved an education the same as every other child. His pain at leaving his mother and her daily torture of listening to his pleading to stay home would not be in vain. The system wanted him; the system could have him and now see it through to the very end; she would make sure Adrian got the education he deserved.

Jocasta decided that she had heard enough from the mouth across the desk. "Mr Cross," she interrupted his incessant droning.

"Yes Mrs Brown?"

"I understand there may be problems with Adrian. I have probably been burying my head in the sand but I want to get him as much help as possible. You are right; he can't be allowed to interact with his classmates if it is going to lead to trouble. Maybe a change of scenery is what he needs. Please do whatever is necessary to help him get on with his schooling."

"Thank you Mrs Brown." Smugness crossed his face and Jocasta could see him mentally patting himself on the back. "We will refer Adrian to special needs and he can start in the unit tomorrow." He handed her a leaflet which gave the address of Adrian's new school placement. "I hope he is happier there than he was here, I really sincerely do."

"Oh I see you've already taken steps to have him removed." Jocasta said accusingly. "I don't know why we bothered with this conversation; it's obvious you already intended to send him away regardless of what happened here." Mr Cross looked down at his desk, seemingly embarrassed by Jocasta's accusations.

"I only want what is best for Adrian, Mrs Brown; I truly believe he will be happier in a specialised unit."

"I'm sure anywhere would be better than here," Jocasta stood up from her chair, "Oh and Mr Cross?"

"Yes Mrs Brown?"

"It's Miss Brown you jumped up prick." Jocasta almost ran out of the door, she could feel her face getting hotter as she walked and knew it must be bright red. Although out of character for her to swear at anyone, Jocasta felt good; it felt right to defend her child.

She went straight to the classroom she had seen Adrian standing in. Looking through the door she saw that indeed it had been Adrian and he was still standing where she had last seen him, sullenly looking at the class before him, not apparently taking part in the school day that played out before him. Jocasta opened the door and walked in, all the children stopped talking and the teacher also looked up at her as she entered. Jocasta walked over to Adrian, took him gently by the hand and walked him out of the classroom without a word. She led him back along the furnace of a hallway, out into the reception area and then out of the school without a backwards glance. Adrian's smile only grew bigger with every step that put space between him and the school he hated so much.

Chapter 6

*'Being a mother is learning about the strengths
you didn't know you had and dealing with fears you
didn't know existed.'*
Linda Wooten.

December 2000
6am

Jocasta woke before her alarm had a chance to
wake her. Having given Adrian the biggest bedroom
- well he had so much more stuff in the house - she
rose from her single bed. The 'value' sheet she had
purchased from Big Value had once again pinged its
way off the corners of her bed. Jocasta carried out her
morning ritual dance around her mattress, pulling at
the corners of the elasticated sheet until finally managing to fit them onto the rectangle of sponge and
spring at her knees. She laid her quilt carefully and
plumped her two pillows up at the head of her bed
before putting on her slippers and making her way to
the bathroom.

Turning on the shower, Jocasta noticed the ever
present blackness on the grout between the once gleaming tiles. No amount of cleaning can compensate for

wear and tear, and because Jocasta spent all her benefits on the things which Adrian required it didn't leave a lot for renovation. She let loose a sigh and allowed herself a moment to assess her face in the mirror.

The mirror and tiles weren't the only things showing signs of wear and tear; Jocasta's face peered back at her through the mirror. Now 37 years old, she was aware she was no longer young and that middle-age was creeping up on her. Her once brown hair was now mostly grey; not such a loss, brown was hardly a colour to cling to. The same dark brown eyes stared back under the now wrinkling hoods and the unibrow had won the fight against hair removal long ago, Jocasta having realised that the only person who cared was her and actually she didn't mind it really. She wondered if her parents had the same feature on their face. If her mother could ever recover from her ordeal to accept her - even if Jocasta *did* look like her rapist father - then perhaps they could reunite and she would find out. Considering her age, she knew it was possible that both her parents were now dead and she may never have the relationship she used to dream of; her mother turning up at her door with her arms open wide waiting to embrace the daughter she could now accept as time had healed her wounds.

Jocasta thought she actually looked better with a bit of age on her, almost as if she had grown into her face. She knew her body was back to being the lumpy potato; days spent waiting for Adrian to come home had made her reach for the biscuit jar regularly, but she felt her age meant that it was ok to be a bit bigger around the middle. There was no one to ask an opinion of so she would keep her own counsel and accept her self-assessed compliment.

Jocasta had spent far too much time gawping at herself in the mirror; she jumped in the shower and quickly scrabbled at her hair with shampoo, allowing the soapy water to cleanse the rest of her body. She needed to hurry, it was nearly time to get Adrian up for school and sort his breakfast out. He was ten now but Jocasta still liked to help him get dressed in the morning, she knew her role on this earth and that was to be a mother to her son.

* * *

7am.

Jocasta walked into Adrian's room. She knew he didn't like the light being switched on as it hurt his eyes so Jocasta walked to the Scooby Doo curtains and pulled them open for him. "Good morning sleepy head," she said and turned to tickle Adrian's foot which was poking out from the quilt at the side of his bed. Immediately she knew that something wasn't right, Adrian's foot felt slick with sweat and hot to touch.

"Adrian, are you alright my darling?" She pulled down the quilt to find Adrian's hair also wet with sweat. Heat emanated from his whole body, it was a tangible extra layer on his skin.

"Adrian?"

"Mummy I don't feel well."

"I know darling, where does it hurt?"

"I don't know; down here," he said, indicating to his lower stomach by rubbing at the bottom of his belly. "I think it's my willy." He was lying on his side in a foetal position, pulling his legs up and rocking as if to relieve a pain.

"Your..." what? That didn't sound like a plausible place for Adrian to have a problem. "Let me see Adrian, let mummy see where it hurts."

Adrian rolled onto his back and weakly pulled at his pyjama bottoms. Jocasta could see how weak he was and realised this was no time to afford Adrian his privacy. She grabbed at his pyjamas and hurriedly pulled them down. Adrian's testicles were swollen; they were turning black as Jocasta looked at them. She held onto a scream, not wanting to scare Adrian.

"Ok Adrian, we need to take you to the hospital."

"Why mummy?" he began to whimper, "What's wrong, why does it hurt?"

"It's going to be ok, they are just a little bit sore and are making you ill darling, I am going to get you some medicine and call an ambulance, you would like a ride in an ambulance wouldn't you?" Jocasta was sure that had Adrian been feeling better he would have protested at the very notion of medicine considering his ability to projectile vomit at the first hint of it, but his quiet acquiescence made her realise this was bad and Adrian desperately needed help. She rushed to make the phone call which would save her baby's life then retrieved the medicine from the cupboard in the bathroom and returned to Adrian's side, pouring the medicine into a spoon, her shaking hands causing more of it to fall on the floor than remain on the metal disc.

Jocasta climbed into the divan bed which had Scooby Doo sheets to match the curtains and the rug on the bedroom floor. She brought Adrian towards her and sat him up as much as she could, stuffing pillows and teddies behind him to prop him up. "Here Adrian, take this." She said as she offered him a spoonful of the pink sticky mixture. She had to push the spoon into his mouth as Adrian hardly seemed to be able to move. His body was actually burning the very parts of skin which Jocasta was touching him with, she realised she would have to let go of Adrian as her embrace would only make him hotter.

* * *

An image of Adrian's funeral played itself in Jocasta's mind as she sat and waited for what seemed like forever. She wouldn't let the funeral parlour dress him, she would do it herself. Jocasta imagined going into the mortuary with Adrian's favourite clothes, no, not clothes, his pyjamas; he was going to sleep for a very long time. She imagined going to the table where he lay and seeing him before her, perfect in her eyes and again she felt the warm enveloping love his appearance evoked in her. Jocasta reaches out to touch her son and he feels hard and cold. Not the warm squidgy loveliness of Adrian but the frozen shell of what he used to be. Despair and a feeling of complete loss makes its way from Jocasta's stomach and works its way up her body causing her to catch her breath. She feels her face beginning to tighten and her eyes to well up. "Stop." She told herself and shook her head to rid the image from her mind.

Looking down on her not dead, still with the living son, she focused on keeping him cool and grabbed a book from his overflowing toy shelves to begin fanning him with.

* * *

A knock on the front door spurred Jocasta into action; she ran to open the door and was met by two men in green. Jocasta let in the two men, who came through the door nonchalantly.

"Hello, what's the problem; we got a call about a child with a temperature?"

Jocasta, even though realising it was a very important factor in Adrian's illness, had not been able to tell the operator about Adrian's testicles; she just could not bring herself to mention it to a stranger over the telephone.

"Yes," she said, "But he also has another problem I need to show you." She led the paramedics to Adrian's room. He still lay on the bed, now naked as

Jocasta had been trying to keep him cool. When the first paramedic entered the room and saw Adrian his whole demeanour changed. This wasn't a run of the mill child with a temperature, this was something much worse.

"Get the bed Tony; we need to get him back to A&E quick." As he said this the paramedic was already picking Adrian up in his arms and moving him out of the flat. "Ma'am we need to get your son to the hospital as soon as possible, please come along with me." As he was saying this, he grabbed Adrian in his arms and walked out of the front door, Jocasta followed, forgetting to collect her belongings as she left and only just managing to remember her door keys so she could let herself back into the flat on her return home. She just hoped that she would be bringing Adrian back with her.

* * *

Jocasta sat, stood and paced in the hospital waiting room, she knew it was twenty steps from one side of the room to the other, there were fifteen blue plastic chairs and they were screwed into the floor. She also knew that it hadn't been cleaned in some time as dust bunnies played amongst the legs of the chairs as she caused a breeze with her constant pacing. Jocasta remembered when Adrian was born here at West London hospital, how he seemed to be dealt with so quickly and returned to her, problem solved. Not this time, this wait seemed to go on forever and was interspersed with terrible recurring images of Adrian cold and dead on the mortuary slab. Jocasta had never felt such terrible grief; it was painful and felt as if claws were tearing at the very heart of her.

Just when she felt she could take no more, the doctor came through the waiting room door.

"Mrs Brown."

"It's Miss."

"Sorry, Miss Brown, Adrian is going to be fine."

"Oh thank god," the rush of relief was giddying in its intensity.

"Yes he will be fine, health wise, but I am afraid I need to discuss his operation with you, please sit down."

They both sat in the cold blue chairs of the hostile waiting room and Jocasta learned that Adrian's testicles had to be removed; the medical term was 'Testicular Torsion', they had strangulated once again and could not be rescued this time. It was necessary, if his life was to be saved, to remove them. She was told Adrian *should* be able to have a normal sex life when he was older but obviously could never have children. He would need testosterone injections as he reached puberty and beyond and when he reached adulthood they could implant silicone testicles so his appearance was 'normal'.

"Well that's alright then isn't it?" Jocasta used her sarcasm often as a defence. Actually she thought it *was* alright. Adrian didn't need to have children when he was older. He had her, they had each other, *she* would love him no matter what. Everything was going to be fine.

Chapter 7

'All women become like their mothers; that is their tragedy.

No man does; that's his.'

Oscar Wilde, The importance of being Earnest, 1895.

October 2003

Adrian had recovered well from his operation with no emotional scars as far as Jocasta could tell. He continued to be educated in the special needs school which was tucked away in Bustle Corner, Elisworth. You wouldn't know it was there unless you had a child in the school, there were no signs to advertise that this was a place the undesirables were educated.

The school seemed to understand Adrian's needs; he had been diagnosed with Attention Deficit Disorder but Jocasta was still of the belief that it was the Education board's way of ensuring Adrian would not be allowed back into mainstream education. She believed that calling Mr Cross a prick had been a huge mistake and he had obviously planted his poison wherever was necessary due to his bitterness towards her.

No matter, Adrian seemed happy where he was. He was not the brightest child; Jocasta knew that; she was no Einstein herself. This didn't worry her; she was managing perfectly well on benefits. Her rent was paid, her house was clean and they had food in their bellies. Holidays only led to trouble; she was a good example of that, so daytrips to the park, free museums and walks around London were holiday enough for them. If Jocasta could support both of them on her benefits then Adrian would easily cope when he left school. It's not as if he had to leave home, Jocasta was prepared to look after him for all of her living days.

* * *

10:22am

The cheap mobile phone Jocasta had purchased from the local supermarket interrupted her daydreaming. It rang with the tone it had been programmed with as Jocasta did not have the internet or any desire to 'download' a new tune onto her phone. She looked at the phone and pressed the button Adrian had shown her she would need to press if the phone ever rang.

"Hello?" she enquired in her best phone voice.

"Hello Mrs Brown?"

Jocasta winced at the mistake but decided not to correct the caller.

"Yes."

"My name is PC Judd calling from Olinsbury Police Station."

Adrian was safely in school so Jocasta knew the call could not be about him. Living on the Fern Bridge it would be no surprise to her if this was another courtesy call advising her to keep her doors and windows secure at night.

"We need you to come to the police station please Mrs Brown; we have your son Adrian in custody."

"In custody, why, what has happened?"

"It's best if we speak about it when you arrive at the station Mrs Brown."

"It's Miss Brown and please, tell me what's wrong? At least tell me if he's alright, has he been fighting?"

"No Miss Brown, not fighting, all I can tell you is it's been alleged he has assaulted a young girl. As he's only thirteen we can't progress with any legal matters until he has an appropriate adult with him. Can you read and write Miss Brown?"

"What sort of question is that, of course I can read and write."

"You would be surprised how many people can't." PC Judd paused, Jocasta thought he may want her to react to that statement in a jocular fashion but *she* did not find it funny so remained silent. "When can we expect you at the station?" PC Judd enquired.

"I can be there in half an hour, but I have to catch the H24. If it's late then I will be longer."

"Ok no problem, in order to save time and reduce Adrian's waiting time, may I ask, do you want us to call a duty solicitor for you or do you have one of your own?"

"Why on earth would I have my own solicitor? I'm not a criminal PC Judd."

"Just doing my job Miss Brown, I'll call you a duty solicitor shall I?"

"Will he need one?"

"It's his right to have one and considering his young age and the seriousness of the offence it would be advisable."

"Fine, then yes please phone one for him. I will be there as soon as I can."

"Thank you, bye."

"Bye." Jocasta fumbled with her mobile phone, not sure if she had pressed the right button to finish the call but there was no sound coming from the earpiece so she assumed she'd got it right. She could feel the beginnings of a headache making its way up her temples. This could not be happening again surely?

A young girl assaulted by her son?

Serious enough for the police to be called and with no prior warning from the school either; it surprised her that they hadn't contacted her first, surely anything that had happened could have been dealt with in the head master's office?

Dazed and confused Jocasta went through her usual motions of leaving the flat; she turned off the television, retrieved her coat and her handbag, made sure all the doors were closed in the flat in case of fire and then went out through the front door, double locking the door as she left. She went down the two flights of stairs and out into the car park, through the children's playground, then walked around to the bus stop on Summervale Road. All the time she was doing this she was thinking, 'Not Adrian, not again, why do they hate him so much? Fucking people, why can't they just leave us alone?' Nothing in her mind made her believe that Adrian was capable of assaulting anybody; he was a sweet and gentle child, persecuted because his face wasn't handsome and his mother wasn't pretty or socially acceptable.

* * *

11:05 am

Jocasta arrived at Olinsbury police station. Although she had walked past it many times whilst shopping in the area and had a quick glance through the window; Jocasta had never actually been inside a police station before. She walked laboriously up the ten or so steps wishing she had made the longer journey up the cement slope which snaked its way up to the door alongside the stairs. Now short of breath and perspiring Jocasta felt she looked a wreck where she had wanted to march into the station calm and dignified. Thankfully the reception area was quiet and Jocasta walked up to the counter, presenting herself in front of the bored looking Asian officer who lounged on a chair, feet up on the desk. When the officer saw Jocasta he removed his feet from the desk slowly and greeted her with a sigh.

"Yes madam, what can I do for you?" he asked.

"I'm here to see my son." Jocasta stated.

"Has he been arrested?" The officer enquired.

Feeling a bubble of shame creep inside her, Jocasta meekly confirmed that her baby boy had been arrested.

"Well I'm afraid they're not ready for you yet madam, you are his mother I presume?"

"Yes."

"Name please?"

"Miss Brown."

"*Miss* Brown." The officer's face was screaming 'typical' at Jocasta only adding to her shame. This was probably one of the only times in Jocasta's life where she wished she *did* have a husband who could come and support her, she felt bad that Adrian was being tarred with a brush that she could not clean. Having no response to his gesture and not knowing what to do next, Jocasta stood meekly waiting for the officer to lead her.

"Ok, well it's just a case of sitting and waiting till they are ready." He told her gesturing to the blue plastic seats bolted to the walls of the waiting room.

"But can't I see him?" Jocasta asked, she couldn't bear knowing he was just a few rooms away from her, "He's only a young boy, he needs me."

"I'm sorry madam; custody areas are dangerous places, no room for people to be hanging around. He is in a cell where he is safe and you are much better off out here safely waiting." He then walked away from the counter, his duty to Jocasta dismissed.

She went and sat in the uncomfortable chair and spent the next hour watching the comings and goings at the station. It was actually quite engaging; an endless procession of humanity walked, marched, ran up to the counter demanding to be dealt with. A car accident, a theft from somebody's car, little Jimmy had set his carpet on fire at home and Jimmy's mum wanted the officer to reprimand him as she 'didn't know what else she could do with the little fucker'. There were people signing on and people signing off and all other manner of stuff which Jocasta had no knowledge of. The officer maintained his bored look, sighing before each sentence and looking as if he carried the whole world on his shoulders. Jocasta couldn't imagine how she would react to having the job he did, but she could understand how such constant pleas for attention would either drive you to become a screaming stresshead or a bored acceptor of your fate.

When even the novelty of watching a day in the life of a station officer started to grate on Jocasta and failed to distract her from worrying about Adrian, she began to pace up and down for what seemed an interminably long time. Finally a man far too well-dressed to be anything other than a solicitor, arrived at the counter and quietly announced himself to the officer as Mr Brown. He was pointed in the direction of Jocasta and he walked over to her, holding out his hand in greeting.

"Mr Brown, no relation." He smiled at her. Jocasta was in no mood to be making jokes, she wanted action, she wanted her son back and she wanted him back fast. Jocasta began to ask Mr Brown a question, but was interrupted by a police officer coming to greet them. How ironic, Jocasta thought, now I want a bit of time, I can't have it.

Introductions were made and finally the officer who introduced himself as PC Judd, walked them through to the custody suite where she found Adrian, looking very much like the little boy he was, sitting on a wooden bench at the back of the room. Jocasta went to him and pulled him into a loving embrace, but he pushed her quite forcefully away and turned his face from her.

"Not here mum." He said to her.

"Are you ok?" she asked him anxiously.

"Yes fine." He said, looking at the floor.

They were led to a high counter - almost shoulder height - where they were looked down upon by a custody sergeant, with a very red face and a round belly fighting to escape the off white shirt which caged it. Sergeant Clarke, read Adrian some rights and entitlements which were lost on both him and her, but Jocasta was confident the solicitor would explain things to her if he felt it necessary. Adrian was then asked some ridiculous questions; "Do you self-harm?" "Do you take drugs?" "Do you ever feel like killing yourself?" Jocasta did not believe that any of these questions were ever answered honestly; who would admit to self-harming, drug taking and attempted suicide, even if they *did* feel like that? *'Oh yes, I stuck a knife in my wrist just the other day officer.'* Ridiculous, she thought.

"Ok, I would like a quick consultation with my client before interview." Mr Brown announced to Sergeant Clarke and PC Judd.

"Yes that's fine, do you need a room or what?" PC Judd enquired.

"No over there is fine," said Mr Brown pointing to the bench Adrian had previously been sitting on and he hustled them over to that area. "Just quickly," he said quietly to them. "I have read the disclosure and it seems to be the girl's word against Adrian's."

"But he hasn't done anything." Jocasta protested.

"Please Miss Brown, I'm sure you're right but we need to get the procedures out of the way." Mr Brown looked at Jocasta over the top of his half-moon glasses. Jocasta relented and he continued.

"When you are in interview I think it would be best for now if you just make no comment. All you have to do is say, "No comment," after everything the officer asks you, ok?"

Adrian nodded; he hadn't yet looked Jocasta in the eye, or allowed her to cuddle him. Jocasta was proud that Adrian wasn't crying. Under the circumstances Jocasta had expected him to be very upset and tearful but he was quiet and respectful; it gave her a small frisson of pride.

PC Judd invited Jocasta, Adrian and Mr Brown though a heavy wooden door, immediately followed by another door, literally inches apart from the first one. They walked into a box-like room containing only a black wooden desk and four chairs; two either side of the desk. By the wall on the desk was an antiquated machine which looked as if it had been well used and abused at the hands of many. Jocasta could not think what it was for, it looked capable of torture. The room had a strange atmosphere, it made Jocasta's ears pop and as PC Judd began to speak, she could hear a slight echoing in her ears, she supposed the room must be sound proofed which caused the anomaly in her hearing.

They all sat down and PC Judd produced two cassette tapes which he removed from their cellophane packaging in front of them. He placed the tapes into the old machine and pressed a button which caused a loud beeping to vibrate around the small room. PC Judd began to speak, "Ok, we are in the interview room at Olinsbury Police Station, I am PC Judd 234TX. It's Friday 10th October 2003 and the time by my watch is 12:46 hours. With me is..."

The introductions continued and PC Judd read from a sheet of paper in front of him, outlining Adrian's rights and again giving the standard police caution.

"Now Adrian, we have had a report from a girl at your school, Charmaine Sprint. Do you know her?"

"No comment," came a muffled reply from Adrian who sat looking at his hands.

"You will have to speak up for the tape please Adrian."

"No comment." Adrian lifted his voice slightly.

"He said no comment." Jocasta tapped the table. "And that's what the solicitor has told him to say, so..."

"Sorry; Mrs Brown?" PC Judd stopped Jocasta.

"Miss." An exasperated Jocasta almost shouted back at him.

"Miss Brown, if you could just be quiet please; you are only here to make sure that Adrian is not mistreated; you are not under arrest and are not obliged to speak."

Jocasta harrumphed and sat back. She was getting more and more agitated as this day went on. Not only were they accusing Adrian of something ludicrous but the procedures they had to go through just to get into a room seemed ridiculous.

PC Judd went on to give full disclosure about the allegation made against Adrian. He informed them that the girl called Charmaine Sprint, who was 11 years old, had been sitting on some steps outside the lunch hall of their school. It was quite a secluded area of the school, not used by many students. Charmaine suffered from Asperger's Syndrome so would sit there often as she liked to exclude herself from the melee of morning break.

When Charmaine returned to her lessons after break, the teacher noticed her top was ripped at the armpit. Charmaine seemed distressed as she was holding her hands up to her ears and rocking in her chair.

"Now, Charmaine was taken out of class and her form teacher spoke to her privately Adrian. She told the teacher that you had approached her on the stairs and without even speaking to her you attempted to kiss her and then grabbed her in the pubic area. Do you know what the pubic area is?"

"No comment."

PC Judd put a piece of paper onto the table and drew the outline of a female form. He then pointed to the groin with his pen. "That is the pubic area, Adrian. I need to know if you understand the area I'm talking about please."

"Of course he does." Jocasta intervened once again.

"Are you happy he understands?" Pc Judd directed his question at the solicitor.

"Yes, I'm happy that your picture is adequate." The solicitor confirmed.

"Ok good, now obviously Charmaine was very distressed, she finds it extremely difficult to express herself especially when she is upset. We are currently video interviewing her in our dedicated suite and all we have at the moment is the statement from her teacher. What we want Adrian is your side of the story." PC Judd paused to watch Adrian's reaction. "This is your first opportunity to give us an explanation; do you want to tell me what happened?"

"No comment." Adrian mumbled, he looked at the floor where his foot tapped against the table leg.

"Adrian wouldn't do that, the girl must be lying," Jocasta said, ready as ever to defend her son.

"Please Miss Brown; you are not here to speak for your son."

"But..."

"You are here to observe that Adrian is being treated fairly but you cannot speak for him."

"It's ok Miss Brown," said the solicitor, "Don't worry, just let Adrian say no comment for now."

It didn't seem right that Jocasta was unable to defend her child when he was in such desperate trouble. She closed her mouth and joined Adrian in looking at the floor. PC Judd went over his initial disclosure line by line, asking Adrian each time, "Do you have anything to say about that?"

"No comment," became the robotic reply. Sometimes Adrian would reply so fast that PC Judd would become agitated and say, "Adrian I haven't asked you the question yet."

It went on in this vein for forty five minutes until the buzzer cut in, informing them the tape was about to come to an end.

"Right I haven't got any more questions, Adrian, do you have anything you wish to add or clarify?"

"No comment."

"Ok, the time is now 13:32 by my watch and this interview is concluded." PC Judd pushed his chair back and walked out of the room without an invitation to follow. Jocasta could see he was frustrated by Adrian's lack of cooperation in the interview. They followed him back into the custody suite and were advised that Adrian would be bailed to return to Olinsbury police station in two weeks' time as they were awaiting the statement from Charmaine.

Jocasta thanked the solicitor who advised her that until Charmaine's statement came through the police didn't really have a case as it was her word against Adrian's. he suggested they wait for the bail return

Mother Be The Judge

date before he went into any greater detail about what may happen to Adrian should he be charged and go to court. Jocasta got the feeling that Mr Brown had dispensed of his duty where Adrian was concerned and was already focusing on his next client. He didn't seem to believe it necessary to go into great length about Adrian's legal rights or to give any assurances about how the case was likely to go; he just moved them out of custody by placing his arm across Jocasta's back and out through reception into the street.

"I will meet you here on the 24th October unless you hear otherwise." Mr Brown said, taking his mobile phone out of his pocket as he spoke. Before Jocasta could ask anything more of him, he had turned his back to her and walked off, talking into his phone.

Jocasta, at last alone with Adrian, looked across at his face. He was eye to eye with her now, no longer the little boy she used to look down upon. His hair was messy and surrounded his face, it was as dark as his father's had been and had the sheen to it that most Mediterranean men had in their hair.

Adrian's dirty blue eyes looked obstinately into Jocasta's own, "What happened Adrian?" she asked of him. "Whatever happened we can work through it."

"It's your fault mum."

This was not what Jocasta had been expecting. Tears, yes, denial, yes, but blame? Where had that come from?

"How is it my fault darling? I know you didn't do this, you just wouldn't."

"I just wanted to know what it felt like." Adrian

shrugged his shoulders and turned away to hide the grin that came across his face. It was not missed by Jocasta however and had someone shoved a knife into her guts at that very moment, it could not possibly have hurt her any more than the nine words her son had just spoken.

"Adrian, please tell me you don't mean that. Tell me you didn't do it, you didn't hurt that little girl." Conscious of the fact they were still in earshot and eye line of the police station, Jocasta began to walk away leading Adrian by the elbow and taking him to one of the benches on High Street.

"Mum, I didn't hurt her; I just wanted to know what a girl felt like. Everybody else has a girlfriend; everybody else has a computer and goes on holiday." He whined as though he had reverted back to being a six year old. "You never give me anything; I never even had a birthday party. I hate you; it's all your fault."

It took a while for her to process what Adrian had said but now Jocasta thought she could see what had happened. It *was* her fault. She hadn't looked after Adrian's needs properly; of course he needed a computer just like all the other kids his age. This incident with the girl was a cry for help, his way of getting attention from her. She believed she knew what she had to do.

"Oh Adrian, I am so sorry, please don't be upset with me. Listen I've been putting money away for emergencies but maybe this *is* one. Come on, let's go to Cambells Electrics and order you a computer. You don't need to worry any more, this is just a glitch. We will sort it out."

She gave him a quick embrace and stepped out in the direction of the electrical store on High Street. She didn't notice the sly smirk on Adrian's face which may have given her a different view of Adrian's true nature.

* * *

20th October 2003

Jocasta opened the envelope with the Metropolitan Police emblem on the top left corner. She felt bile rising into her mouth as the letter opened, this was Adrian's life on the line, the thing that would determine his liberty for the foreseeable future. She unfolded the letter and read its contents.

Mrs Jocasta Brown
731 Summervale Road
Elisworth
West London
TW0 5PV
19th October 2003

Dear Mrs Brown
We write this letter to advise you Adrian Brown's bail conditions have been cancelled. Due to insufficient evidence we have decided to take no further action in this matter.
If you have any personal property at the police station,

please attend with this letter between 9 and 5pm so it
can be restored.
Yours faithfully
PC JUDD 234TX

And that was it, insufficient evidence the letter said. Jocasta knew that *something* had happened because of Adrian's admission but the girl was obviously unable to give a statement; he had been lucky.

She was confident that nothing like this would ever happen again as Adrian was now happily ensconced in his bedroom with his new computer playing a Crime Scene video game which was ironic. It had been an expensive gift considering it also meant a phone line being installed for internet access, but it was worth every penny if it meant Jocasta was doing the right thing by her precious boy.

Chapter 8

'We grow neither better nor worse as we get old but more like ourselves.'
Mary Lamberton Becker

August 2008.

"Happy birthday Adrian, you're an adult now." Jocasta knocked on Adrian's bedroom door; she no longer went into Adrian's room as he had told her he needed his privacy now that he was older.

* * *

Jocasta remembered the day the computer had arrived, she saw it as a boy turning into a young man but was sad to see the bags of Lego, teddies and action men coming out of the room to be replaced with metal, wire and video games.

For the last five years since then Adrian had spent most of his home time in his room. Jocasta insisted he came out to eat meals with her as this was the only way she could spend any time with him. Adrian refused the day trips they used to enjoy together, choosing instead to sit in his room. The only days out they would have together were to the doctor's for regular testosterone injections and to the school for parent consultations. Adrian had also been expected to attend counselling since the incident at the school and although no further action had been taken, the school stated that they had to look after the rights of Charmaine, so asked if Adrian could be relocated to another school. Since then he had had to make the forty minute trek each day to Cranesford. Jocasta had been desperate to accompany her son but he insisted on maintaining some independence and refused any company she had offered.

After Adrian's accusations about having no birthday party, Jocasta had spent the next year saving anything she could, which was not easy as she had now been paying for a phone line. When his fourteenth birthday was imminent she had surprised Adrian with the promise of a birthday party. Adrian, rather than being delighted, had sneered at her and asked just who was he supposed to invite? He told her he spent the day with retards and fuckwits and had no friends, again blaming Jocasta because she had agreed to the change of schools. Jocasta hadn't told him she had had no choice as Adrian was no longer welcome at the school due to his actions towards Charmaine; instead she had apologised and given Adrian the money she had saved so he could buy himself a bike to help him get to and from school each day. He had snatched the money and walked away from her, not bothering to thank her.

The next four years had pretty much gone on in the same way; Jocasta making every effort to meet all Adrian's needs and Adrian barely communicating with her. He would eat his meals in stony silence, offering only grunts in response to Jocasta's cheery conversation before stomping back to his room and shutting the door on any love she offered him.

Adrian finished school at the end of July 2008 and had spent the last month locked away in his room. Jocasta had noticed his skin had become waxen and pale as he no longer spent any time in daylight. She worried he may make himself ill but was pleased on the other hand that he hadn't fallen in with the wrong crowd or taken drugs and got into trouble. She conveniently glossed over the incidents with the young girls; these moments had been banished from her mind to be replaced by only the happy memories of days in London and walks in the park.

* * *

"Are you coming out Adrian? I've got your present out here." Jocasta went back to the living room and sat on the sofa which had still not been replaced. The brown cushions hung from their zips on the back in varying degrees of wear and tear. Jocasta's part of the sofa was heavily dipped from years of sitting in the same position but the other two seats remained plump as no other person had sat on them; Adrian had always lounged on the carpet at Jocasta's feet as a child and had no interest in sitting with her as a teen.

The flat screen television stood proudly on the cheap MDF sideboard, a SKY box beside it, hooked up and ready to go. It was brand new and fully paid for, a result of much sacrifice on Jocasta's part; she had almost forgotten what chocolate tasted like. This was Adrian's gift, his eighteenth birthday present. It was also Jocasta's way of reconnecting with her son; her hope was that now he had reached adulthood they would become companions and she had visions of them sitting together watching the new telly, eagerly following the trials and tribulations of the families on Coronation Street and her personal favourite, East-enders. She knew Adrian had a keen interest in Crime Scenes as he now owned every version of the video game. SKY would now give Adrian the opportunity to watch the programme as well and Jocasta was look-ing forward to learning about and sharing his interest, even if it was a little macabre. She visualised a cosy couple together in a comfortable silence, her in her usual spot and Adrian making his own dent in the sofa.

Hearing Adrian's door open, Jocasta quickly lit the candles on the Victoria sponge she had made the night before. The jam oozed out of the middle and powdered sugar covered the burnt bits on the top. Not being very good at icing, Jocasta had opted for plain and simple. She sat smiling, so proud of the present she had bought for Adrian. Jocasta couldn't wait to see the look on Adrian's face when he saw the television she had bought him. She decided to turn it on so he could see the telly in full effect.

Jocasta heard the flush of the toilet and then Adrian's bedroom door closing once again. Her heart sank when she realised he was not coming into the front room to see her or his present. Believing that maybe he hadn't woken properly yet, Jocasta blew out the candles and sat back to watch This Morning with her favourite, Philip Schofield; he always cheered up her mornings. She would wait until Adrian was ready.

* * *

After another two hours and several unsuccessful attempts to lure Adrian out of his room, Jocasta decided she would pop to the shops to get the ingredients for that night's dinner. She got ready and left the flat, stepping out into the noon day summer's sun. Big Value had built a supermarket behind the Fern Bridge estate which had made shopping very convenient for Jocasta. She enjoyed the short walk through the children's playground to get there as she loved to see the young kids from the estate playing. Her flat looked down on the playground and Jocasta often watched the girls and boys of the estate play with the equipment. The ages of the children would change with the hours of the day; teenagers taking over the playground later in the day, intimidating the younger ones back to their homes. Parents were rarely there to defend their children; the playground was used exclusively by kids from the estate, where everybody knew each other and all were confident their children were safe.

Jocasta walked through the playground now, enjoying the warmth from the sun on her skin. She smiled as she saw two young girls on the swings, kicking their legs backwards and forwards to make the swings get higher and higher. She knew their names were Lacey and Savannah as she saw them here often and had heard them calling out to each other. Jocasta was used to seeing the girls alone but was always filled with disgust for the parents who so carelessly left their children to play. She would never have allowed Adrian to go anywhere alone as a child, especially at the very young age she believed these girls to be; they could not have been more than ten or eleven years old. These parents also seemed to allow their girls to dress like tarts in her opinion. 'What mothers let their daughter wear crop tops and mini-skirts?' Jocasta mouthed to herself. No matter how hot it was if she had had a daughter then jeans and a t-shirt or a pretty summer dress would have been her clothing of choice.

She continued to walk towards Big Value but heard one of the girls calling, "Adrian." She turned to see the girls looking up towards her flat and looked up herself to see Adrian hanging out of his bedroom window. He was smiling down at the girls and threw a paper plane down to their uplifted arms. Jocasta saw the girl whom she thought was Lacey; reach down for the piece of paper. Lacey opened the plane out into its original state and both girls read or looked at whatever was on the paper, giggling to each other. Both girls then waved up to Adrian and skipped out of the park, Lacey still clutching the now crumpled piece of paper. Jocasta looked up again at Adrian's bedroom window hoping to catch his eye and exchange a wave, but he had already returned to the confines of his bedroom.

* * *

Big Value was busy as usual; at times this irritated Jocasta because *people* irritated her. She would often have a trolley barged into the back of her legs as if she were invisible and never a sorry was uttered by the offending trolley pusher. Today though Jocasta didn't mind the crowds; Adrian's refusal to come out of his bedroom had filled Jocasta with a loneliness she didn't believe she had experienced since Adrian had been born. In truth the loneliness had begun to develop ever since the day Adrian had blamed her for his indiscretion with his young classmate. After Jocasta had bought him the computer he had removed himself from her company. Jocasta had been in denial about this though, choosing to keep herself busy tidying the house or preparing for their joint mealtimes, but today's events had led her to realise that even if you have a physical being in your home it can still be a very lonely place. Now she understood what people meant when they talked of being lonely in a loveless marriage.

She meandered down and up the numerous aisles looking for inspiration for a food item which may tempt Adrian from his room. Eventually Jocasta plumped for tuna pasta bake, always guaranteed to make Adrian smile. She went through the checkout and paid for her items then stopped to look at the board where customers would advertise their cast offs for sale. Sometimes a bargain could be had here. As Jocasta looked through the Ads for second hand buggies, cots, toys, furniture and empty fish tanks, she spotted the situations vacant board which was usually empty. Today there was an advert for a position in the store to be a floor assistant. Believing Adrian might be interested and wanting to give him an advantage, Jocasta removed the advert from its slot and put it in her pocket to take home. This could be just the thing Adrian needed to break into the world of work; it may even get him out of his bedroom and onto the sofa. Jocasta left Big Value feeling optimistic about her return home, sometimes more than just household items could be found in the supermarket; this could change Adrian's life.

* * *

Jocasta was thrilled to find Adrian sitting on the sofa when she got home. He had turned on the television and was busy watching a programme about antiques with a decidedly orange David Dickenson rabbiting on about chips. "What do you think?" Jocasta said as she moved into the room, "Its great isn't it?"

"Mmm." Adrian's usual monosyllabic reply came. "Need Sky Plus." He stated before getting up and starting the return journey to his bedroom.

"Well," said Jocasta, "There's a job going at Big Value." She handed him the card. "If you got that you could afford to get it."

Adrian took the card from her hand. He smiled a smile which made Jocasta's heart thump in her chest. "Yeah actually that's a good idea." He enthused, "I'll go there now."

Adrian went and took his jacket from the coat hook, putting it on he then said, "I will see you later." He gave a short wave before leaving the flat.

The job was obviously what had been missing from Adrian's life. Jocasta gave a silent prayer to an unknown God to let Adrian get the job. It pleased her that she had made Adrian smile on his birthday; even if it wasn't with the television she had spent so much money on. Her boy was happy and that's all she needed in her life.

* * *

Putting the pasta on to boil Jocasta sang 'Mama Mia' as she opened a tin of tuna and another of sweetcorn. Food always made her happy. The thought of the flavours entering her mouth, followed by the juicy chew and the satisfying lump in her gullet as the food moved down to her stomach was like sex to Jocasta. Made even more pleasurable by the promise of a pudding, which was a rarity because of the expense. There was pudding today of course and she eyed the Victoria sponge hungrily. "You will be mine, oh yes, you will be mine," she promised the sponge cake. Jocasta eagerly awaited the arrival of Adrian. She hoped it was good news. The meal, the television and a new job would make this the best birthday present Adrian had ever had.

The front door opened just as she set the pasta bake on the table. "I got it." yelled Adrian from the corridor. He came into the kitchen with a jaunty walk and a true smile on his face. "I got the job." he exclaimed.

"Oh that is wonderful Adrian; I knew you would get it."

"Yes, I'm working on the shop floor stacking shelves but if I do well they might put me on the tills."

Jocasta hadn't seen Adrian this animated for a long time. She knew then that he had turned the corner into adulthood and the visions of comfortable nights in watching the new television came back to her. Everything was going to be lovely.

Adrian

Chapter 9

'The wicked envy and hate; it is their way of admiring.'
Emo Philips

December 2000

Adrian woke up after his anaesthetic. A sudden nausea overcame him and he leant over the bed to be sick.

"It's ok darling." His ever present mum was there. She held a paper bowl under his mouth as he vomited and rubbed his back with the other hand.

"How are you feeling now?" she asked him, "Has the pain gone?"

Adrian still felt very groggy, his brain was not working properly but he tried to focus on his penis to see if it still hurt. He did feel sore but the excruciating pain he had felt before the operations had dissipated.

"I think its ok mummy." Adrian said, "It doesn't hurt like before."

"That's good." His mum didn't seem herself; Adrian noticed that she had been crying as her eyes were very red. That was strange to him as she had just said he was going to be ok.

"What's wrong mummy, why are you crying?"

"I was worried about you."

"I thought I was going to be ok?"

"Yes but the doctors told me they had to take away the bit that was hurting." His mother soothed him.

"My willy?" Adrian asked. He was abhorred by the notion.

"No, no don't worry, it's not that. You had the bits below them taken away."

His mother went on to explain everything the doctors had told her, Adrian didn't really understand what had happened to him. He was only ten so didn't comprehend what his testicles were actually used for. His mum told him he would never be able to have children, this was another thing lost on Adrian, he couldn't imagine being an adult so being a father was way beyond his grasp.

"Don't worry mummy, that's ok, I'm feeling much better now." Mother and son sat on the bed hugging each other, Adrian was just glad that the pain had gone away.

* * *

October 2003

Over the next three years it became apparent to Adrian just what he had lost in the operation. As he had started to get older and move towards his teen

Mother Be The Judge

years, he saw the boys at school enter into puberty at various ages. Adrian saw his classmates; some as early as ten years old, begin to get much taller. Almost overnight one lad called Ben had gone from David to Goliath. Voices were beginning to break, much to the delight of the girls in the school who would mimic their sing song voices. Hair grew in the strangest of places and the boys would show each other their thickening penises and pubic hair.

Adrian could not be party to any of this; the removal of his testicles had meant that when he was ready for puberty he should begin to receive testosterone injections to aid his growth. His mother was very much in charge of this destiny and didn't seem to want Adrian to grow; rather than taking him for his injections immediately after he had recovered from his operation she had continued with day to day life and had never mentioned the doctors or injections of any kind. Adrian had badgered her daily and told her that he didn't feel right and wanted to be like all the other boys. She finally accepted Adrian's point of view and began to take him on his twelfth birthday.

It wasn't too late in the grand scheme of boys in puberty as there were a few other boys who hadn't started by twelve, but Adrian felt like he should have been given the opportunity earlier rather than later. He began to resent his mother's involvement in his life; this was a new feeling for him, as a younger boy he had nothing but love for his mum. She was there to catch him every time he fell and he knew she would do anything he asked of her.

After the op, however, he began to wonder why his mum had allowed the doctors to mutilate him in such a horrible way. He had seen hospital programmes on the television and no one had ever had their testicles taken away. Moving on into his teens and wanting to become independent, his mother's love became suffocating.

When his mother had finally taken him to the doctors and the testosterone injections had begun, Adrian could feel the difference to his body almost immediately. The biggest change was the uncontrollable erection that had surprised him the next morning. He tingled from the tips of his toes all the way up to the top of his head. His body, where once was skinny and slightly hairy was now starting to thicken and hair was sprouting from every pore. It didn't happen overnight of course but Adrian felt empowered by his new manhood. He felt whole again.

Adrian then grew and matched the other lads in the class. This pleased him but he was still very aware that something was missing anatomically. After P.E. he would not shower, preferring to be castigated for his smell rather than his lack of bollocks. He would look down at himself each morning and curse the mother that put him in this position.

* * *

Another overwhelming feeling Adrian experienced was a desire for women. Actually, women was not the right word. He definitely preferred younger girls; he liked the fact that they didn't have hair like his hirsute mother. The young girls also seemed to see past his ugliness because they were innocent enough to only seek friendship without any thought of sexual coupling. His looks were irrelevant to them; they only wanted to be his friend. He hoped that he could maybe change their minds as they got older and perhaps start a relationship one day with a nice girl.

One particular girl Adrian liked was Charmaine; she was still very young, looking even younger than her eleven years. He liked her curly blond hair and would dream of putting his fingers inside her ringlets so he could feel how silky they were. She had very bright blue eyes and pale white skin, which was the complete opposite of his mother. She also had a very slender body with no ugly protrusions; just how he liked it. His mother had bits sticking out everywhere and he considered this the epitome of ugliness.

Adrian had tried to speak to her in the playgrounds at break times and lunch hours but Charmaine would never look in his direction, not exchange even a "Hello," with him. Continuous daily advances were spurned and Adrian became increasingly frustrated. He would masturbate furiously at home thinking about how Charmaine may look naked or if she had her mouth around his penis. Adrian felt like the egg timer in his mother's kitchen; it would tick, tick, tick until it finally erupted when the time was right.

The time *was* right for Adrian on the 10th October. He saw Charmaine sitting in her usual spot on the stairs and as he walked towards her he decided just to go for it. He thought Charmaine would enjoy him touching her as he had imagined and anyway she was too stupid to tell even if she didn't like it.

Adrian reached Charmaine and immediately kissed her lips, grabbing at her pubic area at the same time. She had bucked like a frightened rabbit and pulled away from Adrian. Being fearful that Charmaine would run and get a teacher, Adrian had grabbed at her top but it ripped in his hands. Charmaine ran away and Adrian sat on the stairs for the remainder of the break waiting for the inevitable hand on his shoulder which would take him to the headmaster's office.

* * *

Things had taken a different route to what Adrian had expected. Instead of a telling off in the head master's office as had happened the last time he had messed with a girl, police were called and he was now sitting on a wooden bench in the custody suite of Olinsbury police station. Fear permeated every pore of Adrian's body; he had not considered the true consequences of his actions towards Charmaine. His mother had been called and he thought she would be so angry and disappointed with him that he wouldn't blame her if she meted out a very severe punishment.

Mother Be The Judge

He felt like he deserved it, he had been stupid to think that Charmaine would accept him just like that. He realised he needed to *speak* to her first, get her to like him and *then* he would have been able to kiss her.

Once his mother and solicitor arrived and the police conducted their preliminary procedures, it became clear to Adrian that his mother was going to defend his actions. She had arrived and pulled Adrian into her arms, smothering him with her chest and forcing him to smell her vile stench of sweat and hair. She had told him everything was going to be ok and at every opportunity told the police there was no way Adrian could be responsible.

Rather than be proud of his mother's love, her actions caused him to despise her. Didn't she realise he had done wrong?

Didn't she know how much he wanted to do it again?

Couldn't she see that he needed to be punished?

It was her job to discipline and guide Adrian; she shouldn't let him get away with *everything*. Adrian thought all these things but didn't voice them to his mother.

Adrian met his solicitor and when they spoke he could see and feel the contempt coming from him, but when he looked towards his mother she wore the same pathetic look which said, 'Everything's fine, I love you.' Her stupid eyebrow sat atop her piggy eyes. It was one feature which made her so ugly; Adrian had inherited it from her, another reason for him to hate the bloody woman.

He followed the solicitor's instructions and made no comment when asked any questions. He wasn't really listening to the police officer and said, "No comment," where he thought there was a big enough gap between the officer's mutterings.

As Adrian sat looking at his feet he wondered what life would be like with his dad. He knew that his dad lived in Greece and that his name was Avram. His dad didn't know about Adrian because his mum didn't have any contact details for him. Adrian often dreamed about getting on a plane and landing in Greece, his dad waiting on the runway with his arms open ready to embrace his long lost son. Adrian would become a swan in Greece, after being such an ugly duckling in England. He would have never lost his testicles because his dad would have told the doctors to do anything they could to save his son rather than just sign the first form offered to him. Avram and Adrian would live out their days in Greece, dating women and running a bar.

This train of thought continued until the buzzer blasted into Adrian's ears, breaking him out of his day dream.

"No comment." He added, just for good measure.

* * *

Coming out of the police station Adrian waited once again for his mother's onslaught, believing that she may have been acting for the sake of the policemen in her display of unquestioning love for him. He turned to his mother and looked deep into her dull brown eyes.

"What happened Adrian?" she asked of him, "Whatever happened we can work through it."

Rage bubbled up in Adrian's stomach. What was wrong with this dumb cunt? He had hurt a girl for fucks sake. Why wasn't she telling him what a miserable despicable person he was? He decided then to treat her like the mug she was making of herself.

"It's your fault mum."

He could see the look of confusion in his mother's eyes.

"How is it my fault darling? I know you didn't do this, you just wouldn't."

Adrian couldn't believe he hadn't realised what a foolish woman his mother was.

"I just wanted to know what it felt like." And there it was, Adrian could see the pain hit his mother when she heard his admittance. He could almost hear her struggling to come up with yet another excuse for his behaviour. Any minute now he expected her face to change into anger and a punishment to be laid on him.

Adrian couldn't suppress a grin when nothing came. He decided then that he would use his mother's blind love to his advantage and get some compensation for being stuck with such a repugnant mother who had seen fit to butcher him and prevent him from leading a normal life.

Adrian began to whine at his mother about how he never got anything; he thought throwing in a bit about never having a birthday party was a stroke of genius on his part. The ultimate goal here was to get a computer. If he wasn't allowed to touch girls then he knew the computer would at least allow him to look at them. His classmates had told him all sorts of stories about things they had seen online. Knowing their financial situation Adrian had never bothered to ask his mother about the possibility of getting a computer but her display of tolerance today made him believe it possible to get *anything* out of the silly cow.

He had been right. Instead of a punishment his mother apologised to him and took him straight up High Street to buy him the computer he had asked for. Adrian smirked to himself; he was going to enjoy looking at porn, he couldn't wait to start his new life, this was going to be great.

Mother Be The Judge

Chapter 10

'Remorse for what? You people have done everything in the world to me; doesn't that give me equal right?
Charles Bronson

August 2008

"Happy birthday Adrian, you're an adult now." A light knock on Adrian's door hailed the arrival of the Pig, also known as his mother. Adrian's class had been introduced to a thesaurus in lessons one day and after looking up fuck, shit, bollocks and wanker as *had* to be done with any dictionary offered to a young teen, Adrian had perused the book and happened upon 'pig'. The words which followed he believed described his mother perfectly; beastie, creature, fiend, glutton, monstrosity, gorger. All words he could easily associate with that thing he had to live with.

Pig stayed at the door a little while longer, he didn't bother to reply. He had spent the past five years in self-confinement which suited him well. The computer was his mother now. Adrian enjoyed playing Holmes on the machine, working out who committed a crime based on the evidence available. He would spend hours planning the perfect murder, a past time he found others enjoyed also as there were chat rooms dedicated to the pursuit of the perfect crime - bank robbery, murder etc. Adrian liked to imagine that one day his mother would become perfectly murdered, but grudgingly spent time with her to be fed and to get the testosterone injections which were so important to him.

The internet had opened a whole new world to Adrian, not only did he have unlimited access to porn but he had access to porn where girls were 'barely legal' and easily looked young enough to still be in primary school. Adrian also had access to thousands of chat rooms and social networking sites. On the internet he could be whomever or whatever he wanted to be. What also excited Adrian was the fact that every chat room was filled with young girls all desperate to play out their own sexual fantasies. The anonymity of the internet broke through barriers of self-consciousness; no one seemed embarrassed to write dirty things to each other; it was all good harmless fun.

He had seen girls on the webcam taking off their tops and jiggling their tiny boobs at him via the World Wide Web. Adrian had even seen a vagina - not a porn vagina which was obviously over-used and tainted but the virginal vagina of Lacey, a girl who lived on the same estate as him. He knew that in reality she probably wouldn't want to even let him kiss her, but was content with her shenanigans on his computer...... for now.

Pig knocked on the door again, "Just popping out

to the shops Adrian, will get you something nice for your birthday dinner."

"Blah, blah, fucking blah." Adrian muttered to himself. "Go on then, fuck off Pig." He said it quietly as he never let his mother see the real Adrian; that would ruin his manipulation of her. In her presence he was just a moody misunderstood Adrian, persecuted by his peers and in need of his mother's love and protection.

* * *

"Adri-an." A shout came from below his bedroom window. Adrian opened the window and looked down to see Lacey and her friend Savannah standing in the playground below. Lacey was wearing a tiny top and a denim miniskirt. It made her look a lot older than eleven and Adrian didn't like that. He much preferred the dress Savannah had on; it was just long enough for her age but short enough to imagine what was underneath. Adrian quickly drew a love heart on a piece of paper with 'A4L' written inside the confines of the crudely drawn heart. He folded the paper into a paper plane and flew it out of the window and down in Lacey's direction. Lacey picked up the plane, opened out the paper and showed the sketch to Savannah; both girls giggled and then ran off away from the view of Adrian. He glanced up to see his mother gazing up at him from the other side of the children's playground and ducked away quickly so he didn't have to acknowledge her presence there. Adrian hoped Lacey would go online later and give him another look at her fanny.

He decided to go and see what Pig had bought him for his eighteenth. It would be better to open his present while she was out so he didn't have to have her fawning all over him. Adrian went into the living room and looked around for a wrapped gift before noticing the new television on the sideboard. 'And even Sky," he exclaimed in wonder. "Stupid Pig.' He thought, 'As if I'm going to sit here and watch TV with her.' He couldn't resist sitting to watch it though. He was drawn to the dark square and pressed the remote control just to see what the picture was like. Adrian was sucked into an antiques programme with some suited and booted Satsuma gesticulating at him over a piece of crap. Pig walked in and took him off guard.

"What do you think?" she asked him. "It's great isn't it?"

"Mmm." He replied, "Needs Sky Plus." Adrian got up and left the room, he had seen enough old people for one day. The Pig stopped him and showed him a card advertising a job in Big Value. It hadn't occurred to Adrian to get a job before; it was so simple to manipulate the Pig he didn't really need any money. What he did need however, was an excuse to see and talk to Lacey in the flesh. He knew Lacey's mum must go to Big Value and it stood to reason that Lacey must also go there.

Even if Lacey didn't go, it seemed a good way to connect with other young girls. If he could get onto a till then he could even talk to them, get to know them better.

"Yeah actually that's a good idea." He said, "I'll go there now." Adrian grabbed his coat before the Pig could offer to go with him. He rushed off to the supermarket and asked to see the manager there. He was led through to a back room and introduced to a Mr Sprout, an aptly named man for the manager of a supermarket Adrian though. Adrian put on his best behaviour when he spoke to Mr Sprout; unlike his mother, Adrian was able to interact with people. He was quite charming and likeable when he wanted to be; it was his choice to be a loner. It didn't take long for Adrian to convince the manager he was the best person for the job and he was offered a position in Big Value on the shop floor, unpacking groceries.

Adrian walked home sorry that Lacey had left the playground already because he would have liked to have told her about his job. When he got home Adrian yelled, "I got the job." He was feeling in a jubilant mood and decided it was time to give Pig a bone. He would have dinner with her; pasta bake by the smell of it; and eat her stupid cake, then go back to the haven of his bedroom and continue his non-stop trawling of the internet. Life was good, but it was going to get better he thought.

Book 2

Chapter 11

'You not only are hunted by others, you unknowingly hunt yourself.'
Dejan Stojanovic, The Sun Watches The Sun.

ADE234: Are you home yet?

LACE57: yh, just had my dinner :-)

ADE234: Did you like my drawing?

LACE57: Yh, lol A4L 4ever

ADE234: U know I luv u

LACE57: yh but don't know y

ADE234: U r not like the other girls, ure my spcl girl :-)

LACE57: Shut up lol.

ADE234: It's true. What is ure mum doing?

LACE57: She's asleep :0 drunk on the sofa AGAIN she's got dribble coming out of her mouth loooool

ADE234: Is she always drunk

LACE57: Always. I have to do evryfing 4 my bruv

ADE234: That's shit.

LACE57: I know, I can't even go 2 skool every day.

ADE234: That's good lol, I h8td skool, glad I'm done.

LACE57: I've got 6 years left lol.

ADE234: U will do well at skool, ure clever; my clever girl.

LACE57: Ah ure so nice 2 me.

ADE234: Can we play that game again?

LACE57: ??

ADE234: U know, what we did last time :-)

LACE57: No.

ADE234: Come on, u know I luv u xxxxxxx

LACE57: My webcam is not working. I don't like it anyway :-(

ADE234: :-(why don't u like it, its fun.

LACE57: No its not, it's bad. My mum would kill me for doing that.

ADE234: But I luv u, we can be 2gether when u r older, or now if u want.

LACE57: I'm 2 young. My mum sed girls don't do stuff like that.

ADE234: U told ure mum?

LACE57: No, but told her svnnh did it, lol. Shud have seen her face... I'm not doing it again Adrian, its wrong.

ADE234: Oh :-(it's not wrong when u luv someone. Don't u luv me?

LACE57: pmsl

ADE234: y r u laughing?

LACE57: I fink it's funny.

ADE234: Not funny, u r my spesh girl.

LACE57: I'm going now.

ADE234: Lacey don't go, I need 2 spk 2 u.

LACE57: what?

ADE234: Just, I luv u <3

LACE57: Bord now, lol I'm going.

ADE234: Tell me u luv me 2.

LACE57: Shut up lol.

ADE234: Tell me u luv me....................

LACE57: I luv u x

ADE234: R u getting ure webcam fixed?

LACE57: No, mum can't afford it.

ADE234: I'm getting a job at Big Value, I can buy u 1.

LACE57: Can u get me sweets as well?

ADE234: Anyfink 4 my spesh girl.

LACE57: Ok bye.

ADE234: Byeeeeeeeeeeeeeeee DTNO

LACE57: IP x x x x x x

Adrian came off the chat room. He was pleased with his DTNO - don't tell no-one - code and loved that Lacey had made her own, IP - I promise. It had been easy to talk to Lacey online. She was *always* on the computer; things were made easier for Adrian because Lacey's mother was continuously drunk. She could often be seen falling out of Big Value carrying the strongest lager available. Rarely would Lacey's mum be seen laden with bags of *food* shopping or sitting with Lacey in the park; choosing instead to wallow in her alcoholism and to leave Lacey and her younger brother Peter to their own devices.

Adrian would often see Lacey in the children's playground and would watch her as she played.

Although Lacey was young, she never seemed to Adrian to be as carefree as the other kids in the park and she would often be the peacemaker, breaking up the petty squabbles that would occasionally break out amongst the boys when they played Top Trumps with their dog eared cards. On the rare occasion that Adrian saw Lacey without Peter her brother, or any of her other friends, Adrian took the opportunity to make first contact with her.

He had opened his bedroom window and instigated a conversation between them, discussing inane subjects like school and television. At first Lacey was very cool towards Adrian, she would be quite mocking towards him, calling him 'ugly' and sticking her middle finger up at him. Adrian never reacted to anything horrible that Lacey said to him, he would always talk to her and started to throw both Lacey and her brother biscuits and other food out of his window.

One day Adrian had seen Lacey alone in the playground, crying silently to herself as she swung backwards and forwards. Adrian had called to her and they had spoken about Lacey's mother and how she was always drunk and ignored Lacey. Adrian had offered Lacey a much needed shoulder to cry on and after that she would turn up at the playground alone more often and would call up to Adrian's window. It was obvious to him that she enjoyed the attention he gave her; Lacey's giggles and her increasingly flirtatious manner towards him were a good sign she was ready to progress to a relationship with him, in his opinion.

Adrian did not consider Lacey a vulnerable child,

he knew she craved attention and he was happy to oblige. He made friends with Lacey on her Facebook page and soon after that they were privately messaging each other. It was easy for Adrian to say what Lacey needed to hear; she reminded him a little of his mother and her constant need for attention.

It hadn't taken long to cajole Lacey into removing her knickers on the webcam; she would do anything to please him as she believed he loved her and wanted to be her friend. It was the most attention she had been shown in her life and when Adrian had introduced her to his game of 'I'll show you mine,' she played along. Things had gone wrong, however, when Adrian reciprocated the gesture and had shown Lacey his penis. Lacey told him she had never seen a proper one before and she had instantly become different in her manner towards him. The webcam was suddenly broken and she would be more reluctant to chat with Adrian online.

It had taken Adrian a good long week after that to be able to manipulate Lacey into believing he really was her true friend and that he loved her. The airplane love letter had seemed to do the trick because Lacey was back online and chatting to Adrian. The webcam, however, remained 'broken' much to Adrian's chagrin.

* * *

Adrian could feel sexual frustration squirreling

around in the bottom of his stomach. It was an itch he could not scratch, a thirst he could not quench and a hiccough which would present itself in his mind quite unexpectedly at odd moments throughout the day. Adrian could be stocking the cucumbers in his job and suddenly have a full on vision of ramming the cucumber into a hairless vagina. It was a brief moment but it would have a very disturbing effect on Adrian's composure. No amount of porn and incessant masturbation seemed to relieve the frustration which was building steam inside him.

Having no testicles made it hard for Adrian to cum with any vigour; his erection would often get lost mid masturbation leaving him with nothing but a useless flaccid piece of skin in his hand. Adrian felt like he needed something else which would maintain his arousal. He wanted to feel flesh and smell the real smell of a female; he didn't believe it could really smell of fish although his mother certainly kicked up a stench sometimes. Adrian wanted to experience sex in its hot, passionate state. To do something forbidden, he believed, would give him the heightened pleasure he yearned for.

He thought of taking Lacey in his arms and violating her, seeing her face as she at first would be unsure but would then begin to enjoy the pleasure his love would bring her. Imagining what he would do to her allowed Adrian to believe that the hot lava of frustration would work its way up through his body and finally would be able to erupt from him, bringing him the blessed release he so desperately longed for.

Chapter 12

'When the Fox hears the Rabbit scream he comes a-runnin' but not to help.'
Thomas Harris, The Silence of the Lambs

New Year's Day 2009
00:02 hours

Adrian entered his bedroom bleary eyed and stumbled into bed; slightly intoxicated from the Lambrini he had shared with his mother at midnight. She had knocked on his door earlier and begged him to come out into the living room and see in the New Year with her. Considering Adrian had spent most of Christmas Day in his room and had volunteered for every available extra shift at work since then, the Pig had been complaining that she hadn't seen enough of him. This did not bother Adrian in the slightest; he had no interest in his mother's feelings and felt no remorse at leaving her lonely in the flat. He had grunted at Pig that he was busy and tired because he had been working so hard, but she had stood at the door and snuffled like a pig hunting for truffles in the muddy woods. Adrian had relented, more so because he didn't want to hear his mother's caterwauling should she really begin to cry.

He had gone into the living room at 11:30pm and sat and watched a random celebrity do the countdown to the New Year, whilst swigging cheap wine from the bottle. Adrian did not drink alcohol usually and the Lambrini which he had thought was so weak a fish could swim in it; actually had an effect on Adrian making him more forgiving towards the Pig. At midnight he happily grabbed her into an embrace, gave her a quick peck on the cheek and said, "Happy New Year mother." Pig had been delighted, breaking out into a truly terrible screeching rendition of Auld Lang Syne, slurring through the unknown phrases and filling in words with random sounds. This was where Adrian drew the line in his tolerance of his mother and he trundled back to his bedroom to see if Lacey was online.

* * *

Adrian lay back on his bed and closed his eyes for a short while. He instantly felt as though he was on the roundabout from the children's playground and could feel his brain moving around and around, even though his body was incapable of following. The constant swirling made him feel nauseous so he opened his eyes to get his bearings and to ward off the vomit he envisioned would soon come.

He concentrated on looking at his surroundings, hoping to give his brain something else to concentrate on. Adrian decided his room was very boring. He let his eyes wander over the plain grey curtains which hung limply from the white plastic curtain rail. Every other curtain hook had broken due to over-enthusiastic pulling, causing parts of the material to gape away from the rail. Bright white but worn nets gleamed in his window; what his mother lacked in wealth and personality she made up for with her tireless cleaning.

Adrian's eyes wandered down to his feet which were now touching the end of his bed. He hadn't had a new bed since he was moved from his cot into the divan he now lay in. The mattress where once had provided enough spring for Adrian to touch the ceiling as he jumped on it, would now creak in complaint at the slightest movement and the springs had most definitely sprung. Everything in Adrian's room was from the cheapest range in all the relative stores. The only shining opposite to that being his beloved computer, but even that was now approaching six years old and was in desperate need of an upgrade.

Adrian finally felt as if he could sit up on his bed and turned to retrieve his keyboard from the tired computer desk in his room. He leant the keyboard on his knees and sought the private messaging system he shared with Lacey so he could see if she was available online. Five minutes of 'poking' revealed Lacey was offline or ignoring him; Adrian was never sure which it may be ever since the game they had played had put a barrier between them.

He noticed at that moment that Lacey's friend Savannah was online. She would never speak to

Adrian 'in the flesh', but would share a few moments online with him. Unhappily for Adrian the comments she shared with him were usually deriding him for his 'rabbit teeth' or his 'fuzzy hair'. She did not treat him in the same way that Lacey did. Rather than hate her for her cruel jibes, Adrian saw it as a challenge. His ability to manipulate was his one true talent in his mind and he was confident that if he came across Savannah at the right moment then his talent could truly shine. He decided to try his luck now.

ADE234: Hi Sav, what r u doing?

SAV1: Nothing, just sitting in my room.

This was an unusual response from Savannah. It contained none of the usual abuse she would levy at him whenever he attempted to contact her.

ADE234: Happy New Year :-)

SAV1: yh and u

ADE234: Wassup?

SAV1: None of ure business

ADE234: Ok, don't tell me. Did u have a nice xmas?

Adrian waited for a response from Savannah. He knew she was online because there was a green dot next to her name on the messaging list. After about five minutes he decided he was going to stop waiting and go to bed; the wine was still having an effect on him and he was tired. As he turned away from the screen a bong sound alerted him to Savannah's response.

SAV1: I h8 my parents.

ADE234: Y??

SAV1: They had a big ruck on xmas day. My

stepdad smashed evryfing, even my Nintendo.........

ADE234: Oh no, y did he do that?

SAV1: Bcos he's a wanker. My mum didn't care, they just argue all the time, all they care about is there beer.

ADE234: Oh

SAV1: And drugs. I saw my stepdad put a needle in his arm ffs.

ADE234: They luv u tho, don't they?

SAV1: NO, NO, NO............ they don't luv me, they wudnt care if I was dead. I'm gonna kill myself.

ADE234: Don't do that Sav

SAV1: Y not? No 1 wud care.

ADE234: I would care.

SAV1: Really?

ADE234: Yh, I like u.

SAV1: But I am so horrible 2 u, y do u like me?

ADE234: I don't care about that, I really like u :-) I don't want u 2 die.

SAV1: Well I don't know what I'm gonna do. I feel like shit. :-(

ADE234: Do u need a cuddle ()

SAV1: Yh, lol, thnx

ADE234: What r u gonna do now?

SAV1: I don't know.

ADE234: Do u wanna have a drink? I've got some wine.

SAV1: I'm not sppsed to go out.

ADE234: Thght you didn't care about ure parents and you h8td them?

SAV1: Yh ure right. I'll come out, shall I call at ure window?

ADE234: No, I'll come and meet u, we can have some fun away from the parents :-) <3

SAV1: Ok, where?

ADE234: At the allotments.

SAV1: Ok.

ADE234: U shd delete this so ure parents dnt know where uve gone.

SAV1: uh ok, c u in a min. :-)

* * *

Adrian felt lucky; communication with Savannah was completely unexpected and now only a short conversation later and he was on his way to meet her. He had sneaked out of the flat; his mother had not quite made it to bed, he had seen her foot dangling off the sofa and could hear the television still playing in the confines of their front room. Slipping silently out of the front door he crept down the communal stairs and let himself out of the communal door, ensuring he caught it before it could slam shut and helping it to click silently closed.

The weather was very good for New Year, it was crisp and dry and Adrian could smell the sulphur in the air from the exploded fireworks which had lit up the sky at midnight. He kicked the odd empty fallen rocket as he walked through the children's playground. Moving briskly on the pavement, excited by his imminent meeting, Adrian made his way past Big Value and on past the gargantuan rugby stadium which sat proudly in Elisworth but declared itself as 'Twockford'; something most of the local residents were also prone to do as Twockford was a more affluent area, boasting residents with Class.

He looked up at the stadium awed by its presence in an otherwise residential area. It seemed strange to walk past houses and parked cars only to find this expanse of concrete and glass waiting for the arrival of the chanting crowds on rugby days.

As Adrian neared the dual carriageway he took a detour down an alleyway used only by the keepers of the allotments which were tucked away behind a line of bushes on the road. Adrian and the other kids in the neighbourhood had frequented these allotments on many occasions. The other kids to pull up plants and allow the pet rabbits and chickens to escape which would provide them with short term amusement before seeking pleasure elsewhere; Adrian generally went there to be alone in a different setting, away from the claustrophobic love of his mother and away from his life in general. He liked to see how tomatoes would develop and wondered at how strawberries went from small white flower to hard green nubbin into sweet and juicy red deliciousness. Adrian had spent many hours in these allotments and knew them well. He knew which squares were cultivated regularly and knew which ones had been abandoned. Adrian had actually put his name on the waiting list for an allotment when he had turned eighteen and was currently saving for a shed to put on the land when he finally got a plot. He had longed for a place where he could sit without the inevitable interruptions from his mother.

One particularly well kept allotment which Adrian admired the most, boasted a blue painted shed with ornaments hanging from it; a squirrel, a robin and some butterflies. It also had a cast iron bench proudly displayed on a slab of concrete in front of the shed which Adrian would often sit on when the owner wasn't there. Adrian sat on the bench now to await the arrival of Savannah. He took out the Lambrini he had lifted from the corridor of the flat on his way out, opened it and took another swig while he waited. It was now about one o'clock and Adrian was feeling tired. He put his head back and fell asleep almost immediately.

* * *

"Adrian, wake up."

Adrian awoke to find Savannah pushing him gently on the shoulder.

"Adrian you doughnut, you fell asleep." Savannah giggled.

"Eh? What's the time?" Adrian asked.

Mother Be The Judge

"Half one, I had to run here, it's well dark outside and there was some weirdo standing on the corner."

"Did your mum and stepdad see you go out?"

"'Course not, like they'd let me out at one o'clock in the morning." Savannah sighed, "I don't know why I came here to see you anyway." She sneered at him.

"Well why did you come then?"

"I don't know, I'm pissed off with them fucking people. They always argue; I hate them. Every fucking Christmas I have to see them like that."

"Only at Christmas?" Adrian smirked. Savannah smiled at him, "Nah," she said, "Every fucking week."

Adrian didn't like Savannah swearing, it made her seem a lot older than her young years and he didn't think it sounded right coming out of her small delicate mouth. All the kids on the estate swore though; practically the minute they could *talk*, a tirade of fucks and bollocks would escape their mouths whilst at play.

"Where's Lacey?" asked Adrian.

"She's gone to her nans, not coming back till school starts. She hates it there; her Nan hasn't even got Sky." An incredulous Savannah answered.

Adrian now understood why Lacey had not returned his messages. It made him feel good to know she hadn't given up on him.

"Have you kissed Lacey?" Savannah sang, her eyes twinkling. Adrian didn't reply, he was surprised that Lacey had told anyone about their communications. He had expressly told her not to tell.

"No," he replied, "Did she say I had kissed her?"

Savannah shrugged her shoulders and looked

away. "Nah, I just know she likes you." She turned back to look at Adrian. "And I saw that letter remember, don't know why she likes you, you're ugly."

"Well you aren't ugly Sav, you're very pretty."

"Really?" Savannah seemed surprised. It seemed no one had ever told her this before.

"Yes Sav, I love your hair." Adrian reached out to touch her shoulder length chestnut hair. In truth it was always dirty and hung in rat's tails around Savannah's face. Adrian could actually see a creature making its way through the tangles as he touched it.

Savannah moved herself out of Adrian's reach, "Get off." She admonished him, "You're not my boyfriend, where's the wine?"

Adrian produced the bottle of Lambrini, twisted off the cap and took a long gulp from the bottle neck. He passed the bottle to Savannah who took a hefty swig and screwed up her face afterwards, bringing her hand up to her mouth as if to keep the wine in.

"Have you had wine before?" Adrian gestured towards the bottle in Savannah's hand, "Do you like it?"

"I've had WKD before, that's much nicer, this tastes like piss." she exclaimed.

"Yeah but it gets you pissed." Adrian laughed.

Both Adrian and Savannah sat on the bench alternately swigging from the bottle and talking with each other. Adrian encouraged Savannah to talk of her problems with her family, she had been reluctant at first but the wine gave her courage and soon her sorrows were flowing. Adrian consoled Savannah with his words and ensured she had a good share of the litre bottle of wine. As time wore on Savannah became less hostile towards Adrian's advances which began once again with hair touching, arm touching and moved on to Adrian putting his arms around her to 'keep her warm' in the cold dark allotment.

Adrian brought his face closer to Savannahs. He was so close he could feel her breath on his face, it smelled of the sweet wine she was drinking. He could see her small white teeth twinkling in her mouth as she opened and closed it whilst talking. Adrian was overcome with an urge to kiss Savannah. Mindful of Charmaine's reaction to him grabbing her in the past, he resolved to take his time with Savannah. He was determined that this time he was going to get what he wanted.

Savannah's intoxication made her oblivious to Adrian's advances, she was a naturally tactile person and as she became more comfortable in Adrian's presence she didn't mind him consoling her.

"I really like you Savannah." Adrian whispered.

"Do you know what Adrian?" she slurred, "You're alright too." She knocked back the last dregs of the wine bottle and marvelled at the now empty vessel. "Cor we drunk all of that." she exclaimed.

"You drunk most of it," laughed Adrian.

"Oh," she giggled, "Can you get any more?"

"No."

A melancholy came over Savannah and she sat back, apparently reflecting on her problems. Both sat quiet for a short while and Savannah began to shiver;

her body temperature dropping due to the alcohol coursing through her veins.

Adrian put his arm around Savannah once more and she leaned into him, enjoying the warmth his embrace gave her. Without words Adrian lowered his mouth to match Savannah's. She knew he wanted to kiss her and felt that she may like to kiss him as he had been so nice and seemed to understand her so well. Savannah reached for Adrian's mouth with her lips. Adrian became immediately excited at the feel of Savannah on him. He forced his tongue into her mouth, which made her pull back from him. "It's ok, this is what everybody does." He assured her. "It's nice Sav, you're nice."

Savannah shivered and Adrian pulled her closer, he could feel his erection pushing its way through his trousers and his body was starting to take control of the situation. Even though he knew it was wrong he saw his own hands reaching for Savannah's clothing and start to travel towards her immature breasts, still braless under her t-shirt. Adrian did not seem to have any control over what he was doing, it was as if he were looking through a window at a scene playing out in front of him; a type of surreal porn. Adrian watched as he held Savannah down, pinning her arms to the bench. He watched her fall to the ground and to kick out with her legs and then saw himself grab those legs and force them open, pulling at her jeans and knickers, ripping them off with his free hand. Adrian could feel his own hand take his penis from his trousers and then insert it into Savannah's vagina. He became lost in his emotions and in feeling her hotness, holding her by the neck as he had seen happen in the films he had watched online. He could hear only a rushing sound in his ears and was blinded momentarily as he pumped furiously into Savannah's body.

Adrian felt himself come back to his senses after a short while, once again his erection had begun to fail and the emotion which had overtaken him just moments earlier began to dissipate. He looked at Savannah's face which seemed to him to be very peaceful. She wasn't screaming or crying, her eyes were closed and he thought she must be enjoying herself. As he looked closer he saw his hand was still holding Savannah's throat and her two little hands were gripping the sides of his fingers.

Adrian snapped back into his body and mind. He could feel he was whole again and he withdrew himself from the ground where Savannah lay. Looking down at her body now gleaming white, legs naked and twisted against the concrete slab; he called her name. Her eyes remained closed and she did not respond to him. Adrian put his ear to her chest to see if he could hear or feel her breathing then slapped her hard on the face to try to get a response from her. She did not move. Nothing of her moved. She lay cold and still and silent on the floor at Adrian's knees. She was dead, he had killed her.

* * *

Still and silent; everything surrounding Adrian had come to a standstill. Even the wind had stopped its motion through the leaves of the trees surrounding the allotments. Birds which had begun to twitter in the coming morn had stopped their chattering and car engines were no longer audible in the allotment. Adrian viewed Savannah as though at the end of a camera lens; his whole being focused on her lifeless face. From one moment of maddening passion came this cold lifeless angel before him. Adrian thought Savannah really did look like an angel now; it was almost as if death suited her. He spent a moment pondering the beauty of her but could feel truth creeping its way into his bones.

The truth was he had just raped and murdered a young girl. Adrian was surprised at how normal he felt about his situation. Her death did not upset him, he was calmed by it. The only panic he felt was in the being caught and having to go to prison. He had been silly not to plan this better and chided himself for getting caught up in the moment and carrying out his plan; one, at the wrong time and two, on the wrong person. He had been planning Lacey's demise for weeks, hoping the murder would be the edge he had needed to give him the release he required. He was disappointed that that had not happened and believed that he still needed Lacey as he had a real emotional connection with her.

Adrian gave silent thanks for the crime scene games he had played tirelessly since the computer became his. He began to view the scene before him as a chapter of the game he knew so well; DNA, finger-prints, hair samples. He knew he had to get Savannah to running water to clean her up and that he had to dispose of her clothing in case he had left any trace evidence behind. He took one last long look at Savannah, stroking his hardening penis as he did so. He thought he may as well make use of her while he had her. The night was nearly over and he resolved to get to work, he had a lot to do in the next few hours.

Chapter 13

'Love is blind.'
William Shakespeare

New Year's Day
06:00 hours

The sound of the front door woke Jocasta from her snoozing. She had not moved from the sofa since she had settled there after seeing in the New Year with Adrian. Jocasta looked at the clock and wondered where Adrian was going so early in the morning.

"Adrian, you're up early, where are you going?" she called out to him.

"Nowhere, I've just been out for a walk. I felt a bit sick after that wine." Adrian called back to her. She looked into the hallway to see Adrian's trouser bottoms were wet up to the knees.

"Have you been jumping in puddles?"

Adrian didn't respond to her question, instead he went into the bathroom and locked the door.

Feeling the empty hunger in her stomach which comes after a night of alcohol, Jocasta got off the sofa and went into the kitchen. She began to make herself some tea and toast. She pulled out the cheap white toaster she had bought many moons ago. Jocasta wondered why the people who made toasters had never made the slots big enough for the slices of bread. She had tested various loaves of differing sized slices and was yet to find a piece which fit the toaster. As she was making the decision between three quarters toast, a quarter raw or turning the toast mid-cook, Adrian came out of the bathroom wrapped in his threadbare towel. He had his dirty clothes in his hand and walked them over to the washing machine.

"Adrian I'll do that." Began Jocasta, she had been waiting for enough clothes to make a load and did not want him ruining her system.

"No I need them for work tomorrow; I'm putting them in now." Adrian stuffed the clothes in the machine and set the dial to its highest temperature.

"That will shrink your clothes." Jocasta exclaimed, but Adrian just ignored her, stomping out of the kitchen and into his bedroom. Although Adrian often confined himself to his room, Jocasta found his behaviour odd; he almost never went out for a walk although she could do with some fresh air herself after overindulging in the wine last night. She could excuse the walk but wondered why his legs had been wet and why he felt the need to shower and wash his own clothes. Still, she thought, it's nice that he had made such an effort with her at midnight and she believed maybe all of this was a sign he was becoming an adult.

Jocasta was optimistic about her future relationship with Adrian; maybe the nights in front of the television were not such a pipe dream after all.

Chapter 14

'What should I possibly have to tell you, oh vulnerable one? Perhaps that you're searching for too much? That in all the searching you don't find the time for finding.'

Herman Hesse Siddhata

New Year's Day 2009
19:00 hours

PC Tom Hunter stood at the front counter of Olinsbury police station. It had been a long five hours since he had started his shift at two o'clock and he had already taken three crime reports; one for theft from motor vehicle and two credit card deceptions. He had also seen countless people who were prepared to spend three hours queuing just to ask him a question or produce their documents to him. He just couldn't understand how on a Bank Holiday people were prepared to give up their precious time and visit a police station of all places. He could think of much better things to do with his time, namely drinking copious amounts of alcohol down the pub with his mates.

Tom wondered where his relief was; he was Hank Marvin Starvin' and wanted a pee. As he was about to go on the radio to request his break a couple walked in through the glass front door of the station. PC Hunter completed his usual assessment of newcomers to the station, after deciding they may need the fashion police rather than the real deal, he noticed the woman was in a highly panicked state. Her hair was in wild disarray and Tom could smell alcohol on her breath as she drew nearer. The fellow didn't look much better; he was glassy eyed with the dulled look akin to heroin addicts. He also smelt of alcohol and Tom could feel another domestic crime report coming on.

"Hello, how can I help you?" Tom asked, fiddling with the handcuffs on his utility belt, he wondered how long it would be before he had to use them.

"Please, my baby is missing." The woman said, leaning her head against the safety glass which separated her from the rest of the station. She let loose a wail of desperation,

"My baby, please, please." She cried.

The male who was with her took her by the shoulders. His movements were slow and deliberate and he was obviously concentrating on keeping upright. He leant on the woman and said, "Come on Mae, calm down. It's going to be ok. She's just gone to her friends or something."

"Get off me." She screamed at him, "Just fuck off Mike, you don't know fuck all, you're too stoned, you are always fucking stoned. Fuck off." She pushed him back into the blue plastic chairs and he sat down, no longer capable of restraining her.

Tom gestured to the woman. "Madam, please

come back to the counter and tell me what has happened." He could tell this was no run of the mill domestic and if a child was missing he needed to take the details and get the child's description circulated on the radio as quickly as possible so that the policemen on the street could start looking for him or her.

He buzzed the woman into a smaller room where they had a desk and a computer and he could speak to her more intimately than from behind a glass screen.

"Ok, start with your name, what is it?"

"Mae West."

Tom lifted an eyebrow.

"It really is." She put her hand to her mouth and gave a large sniff. Tom could see this was no time for jokes so continued with his questions.

"Ok, tell me what happened." He said, taking out his notebook so he could record any salient points.

"It's my daughter Savannah, I got up this morning and she wasn't at home."

"Ok, when was the last time you saw her?"

"About 11 or maybe 12, I don't know, I was asleep on the sofa; maybe 12 or 1 this morning." Mae began to cry again. "I don't know where she is, please; you have to find her, her brother needs her."

Tom took all the details about Savannah. Mae told him that there had been a big argument and the drug addled boyfriend currently sitting in the waiting room had smashed all of Savannah's things as well as most of the household objects. Mae had been pretty hazy about events after that as she had been drunk, but she was able to tell Tom that after finding Savannah missing she had made several attempts to find her at her friend's houses only to come up empty. Tom thought Savannah may be hiding at a friend's having had enough of her parent's drunken antics and had probably asked her friends not to say she was there. Although she was only eleven years old, Tom knew the estate she lived on and knew children from that estate grew up a lot quicker than a conventional child.

"OK Mae, sit tight here and I will go and circulate her as missing. Every police officer on borough will be looking for her, I'm sure we will get her back for you soon enough."

"Ok, can I go and have a fag?" Mae enquired.

"Yes, by all means go outside and I will come back and get you when I need you." Tom showed Mae out into the main reception area once again and made his way to the first floor control room. Once there he circulated Savannah's description to all officers on duty.

"Please be aware of a MISPER by the name of Savannah West. Female, IC1, 4'10", shoulder length brown hair, brown eyes, slim build, believed to be wearing a white t-shirt and jeans with grey UGG boots and a black puffer jacket. No jewellery, no marks, scars or tattoos."

Tom then went to let his Inspector know about the missing child before completing his report on the MERLIN system which he so hated. As he typed he contemplated how long it may be before he ate again. It irked him that he may now be spending a good hour on a report that would probably go nowhere as Savannah was more than likely ensconced in a friend's bedroom playing the Xbox and calling her parents every name under the sun. With any luck he would get a call before he had done most of it letting him know she had been found.

* * *

19:45 hours

PC James Mann received a call on his radio asking him to attend 824 Summervale Road, Elisworth, to make enquiries about a missing girl named Savannah West. He took the call and made his way on foot to the address. James had been a Safer Neighbourhood Officer for twenty years and the Fern Bridge Estate had been his local beat for the last ten. Countless calls to missing children often came to nothing. Most of the time it was teenagers throwing tantrums or neglected kiddies that had walked away from their ignorant parents who were too busy chatting to notice their little one had wandered off. James didn't believe this call would amount to much more than this so took his time to walk to the address. He was on the lookout for a local scrote named Daniel who had been stealing bicycles by the dozen and selling them on for paltry amounts. He knew it was Danny, every instinct he had told him this, he just needed to catch the little sod at it.

James walked the long way around the Fern

Bridge in the hope of spotting Danny but there was no sign of him. Arriving at 824 he hoped the parents had arrived back from making their report at the station as he didn't want to spend any more time than he had to at this address. Waiting in someone's garden for them to return home was not his idea of time well spent. In the absence of any door knocker or bell he knocked on the glass panel of the front door to 824. He immediately saw a woman come out from an inside room and rush to the front door.

"I've just got home." She said as she invited him in. "I don't know why you need to come here; you should be out looking for her. If she was here I would know." The words tumbled out from the woman's mouth and tears streamed down her mascara streaked face.

"We have to check the house Mrs?" James had forgotten her name already as he was still wondering what Danny was up to.

"West."

"West, yes, we have to check the house, you would be surprised how many kids are found hiding under the bed or in a wardrobe somewhere." Or dead in the attic he thought to himself.

"Well she aint fucking here." Mae said sarcastically, "Do you really think I've spent all day looking for her and I wouldn't bother looking for her in her own fucking room?"

"Mrs West, I know you're upset and worried about Savannah. We have our own way of investigating missing children and more often than not it is the best way to find them. Just let me get on with it and then we can concentrate on looking for Savannah elsewhere." James moved into the hallway. "Now have you got any of her friend's details here and I will need a photograph as well please."

"I don't know," Mae floundered, looking around her hopelessly, "I must have a photo somewhere."

"I haven't introduced myself, I'm PC Mann and I'm your local bobby, have we ever met before?"

James began to manoeuvre Mae deeper into the corridor so he could gain access to the living room. As he arrived at the room he spotted a dishevelled male sitting on the edge of a bright blue sofa, scrabbling at cigarette papers and a suspicious looking wrap on the coffee table. James did not want to lose focus on his investigation so stored that information in his mind; should the MISPER come to nothing, an arrest for possession would be good for his figures.

James moved around the front room, wading through broken ashtrays, discarded beer cans and other detritus. Mrs West had obviously not had time to clean before his arrival; he wondered if she actually *ever* cleaned, the place was so messy. He looked under the smoked glass dining table, moving the chairs out of the way so he could get a good look underneath.

"I think we would know if she was under there." Mae commented, throwing herself onto the sofa and looking at her partner in disbelief.

Unperturbed and determined to do a thorough job, James continued to make his way around the two bedroomed flat. Followed by Mae he did kitchen, toilet, airing cupboards and main bedroom before concentrating his efforts on the second smaller bedroom which Savannah shared with her brother Andrew who was currently sitting on his bed watching Ben 10 on a small flat screen telly.

"Hello," said James.

"Five-oh need to check the room Andy, go in with Mike so he can have a good look." Mae's slang was not lost on James, even in the event of her daughter going missing he marvelled at how she was determined to sound 'cool' in front of her young son. The young lad got off his bed without a word and left the room.

"Has Savannah got a computer?" he asked.

"Yeah she's got one of those notebooks," said Mae; reaching under a pillow and coming out with a small black square. "It's Pay as You Go; I don't know where the dongle is though." She said, returning her hand underneath the pillow but this time coming up with nothing.

"Ok, if we need to look at it we can seize it later and get a lab to take everything off it," James informed her.

"Can you do that?" asked Mae.

"Yes most things as long as they have been saved to the computer's hard drive at some point. It's amazing what they can do nowadays." James continued to look around the small cramped bedroom, it didn't take long for him to establish Savannah was definitely not there and he left shortly afterwards, advising Mae the police would do all they could to find her and reminding her to call the station if Savannah came home in the meantime.

James left the flat and got onto his personal radio to let the controller know how he had got on.

"Tango x-ray receiving 175?"

"Go head 175."

"Yeah I've done a full search of the flat, no sign of MISPER, can you let the Guv know? Over."

"Yes received, thanks for that, over."

"No problem, over."

James went off on his eternal hunt for the elusive Danny, all thoughts of Savannah West now gone from his mind.

Chapter 15

'What we find changes what we become."
Peter Morville

2nd January 2009
09:00 hours

"Good morning, an eleven year old girl has gone missing from Elisworth in West London."

Jocasta heard her hometown mentioned on the morning news. She stopped the ironing she had been doing so she could listen more closely to what had happened.

"Savannah West has been missing, it is believed, since around midnight on New Year's Eve."

Jocasta gasped when she saw the picture of little Savannah come onto the screen. She knew this little girl, it was the one who lived just around the corner and played often in the playground outside their flat.

"Adrian" she called, "Adrian, come and see this."

"What?" Adrian asked as he walked into the room.

"A little girl has gone missing, look it's Savannah. You know her don't you?" Jocasta watched Adrian move towards the television and touch the picture on the screen. He then went to sit on the sofa, looking intently at the unfurling report in front of him.

"Savannah was last seen at her home on New Year's Eve, wearing a white t-shirt, blue jeans, black puffer jacket and grey UGG boots. Her mother and step-father have been questioned and intend to start a search from their home estate, the Fern Bridge estate in Elisworth. It is hoped that people from the local area will volunteer to help search for Savannah. People are asked to visit their local news website for more information."

Adrian jumped up from the sofa. "I'm going to help them look for her." He announced.

"Why Adrian," Jocasta asked, "Don't you have to go to work today?"

"Yeah but mum, she's missing. Everybody should help, even you; get your coat and we will go and find out what's going on."

Thrilled by the prospect of spending time with Adrian, even if it was in the direst of circumstances, Jocasta immediately got her coat. She saw Adrian return to his bedroom, leaving his door open. She took that as an invitation to follow him into the room and went in to find him looking at his computer. He appeared to be deleting something as after pressing a few buttons his screen went blank. Adrian looked up to see Jocasta looking over his shoulder.

"What are you doing?" he snapped at her. "You shouldn't be in here."

"I just thought you were coming with me. Sorry

Adrian, I wasn't being nosey, what are you doing anyway?" Jocasta edged forward to see if she could get a better look at what was on Adrian's computer.

"Just looking for the News about Savannah; I want to know where they are searching for her." Adrian brought up a 'Local News' web page and clicked on a link which took him to information about where a search for Savannah was being conducted.

"They are meeting at the Community Centre at 10 o'clock," said Adrian, "Come on, let's get down there."

Jocasta hadn't seen Adrian so animated for a very long time. She was proud of him. It was nice to see he cared that Savannah was missing and she was pleased Adrian was making such an effort.

They met with a large group of people. Jocasta recognised Savannah's parents from the News report and a lot of faces that she had seen about the estate before. A policeman with a loud hailer stood up on a block of concrete; Jocasta recognised him as the policeman who often patrolled the streets of Elisworth.

The officer waved his arms to get everybody's attention. People eventually stopped their individual conversations and turned towards the officer on the makeshift podium.

"Good morning ladies and gentlemen, I am PC Mann from Olinsbury police station. Thank you all for coming here today. There are leaflets being handed out, please pass them out to each other. They have Savannah's picture on so you all know what she looks like. Now we would like you all to split up and go down every street, every alleyway, into every park and playground. Search bushes, bins, sheds and anywhere else you can think of. Savannah has been missing for more than twenty four hours now. She will be cold and hungry. Let's do what we can to get her home to her parents."

A few people began to clap but quickly stopped when others threw them incredulous looks. PC Mann switched on his loud hailer again.

"Oh just quickly, sorry," he said. "If you find Savannah, please call me on the number on the leaflet or call one of the officers listed on there. Right let's go."

Jocasta grabbed Adrian's elbow. "Where are we going to look for her Adrian?" she asked him.

"I'm not going with you mum, you walk too slowly." Said Adrian; much to Jocasta's dismay.

"But Adrian..."

"No mum, you should follow those people over there. They are going around the estate. I'm going with this group; they are going to the allotments."

Jocasta was upset that Adrian didn't want to walk with her. She had only agreed to go with him because it might mean they would spend some time together and now she had to traipse around the estate with people who never acknowledged her, to look for a girl she didn't really care about, although she did hope that they found her quickly, Eastenders was on tonight and she really wanted to know what was going to happen to Roxy who had just been driven into a frozen lake.

Adrian wasn't panicking about Savannah being found. He knew her body would come to light at some stage and decided he would like to be in control of when that might be. When he saw the expected News reports on the television, it pleased him that the Wests had jumped on the media bandwagon and had decided to hold their own search rather than allow the police to do their job.

Knowing where he had hidden Savannah's body, Adrian knew he needed to be on the search team which went over to the allotments, so on reaching the crowd; he kept his ears open to ensure he knew which groups were going where. He didn't want to be distracted by his mother wittering on in his ear so made sure he directed her to another search team.

When his group of searchers - which included Savannah's step-father - set off, Adrian was at the front, leading the group at a brisk pace. Whilst walking along the streets to get to the allotments, Adrian made a big show of looking in hedges and calling Savannah's name. The groups were followed by several media companies all hoping to be present when Savannah was found alive or dead.

About fifteen minutes later, Adrian's group entered the rusted gates of the allotment. Adrian had been speaking to Mike, who told Adrian he had been called by countless newspapers and was currently sorting out a deal to sell his story. He told Adrian that even if

Savannah was found alive he still stood to make at least ten thousand pounds out of it. Adrian was actually disgusted by Mike's attitude towards Savannah's situation. He realised he actually thought a lot more of Savannah than her own family. He decided he had probably done her a favour and saved her from a life spent in misery.

The group comprised of around six people if you didn't include the media who were happy to observe and report about the search rather than actually take part in it. Adrian turned to the group and began to direct them to different corners of the allotment, suggesting they all meet back at the gates once the search was completed. Adrian headed off in the direction of the stream which ran behind the allotments. He was followed by his new found friend Mike who was rolling yet another cigarette. Adrian called out, "Savannah." A few times, Mike lit the cigarette and kicked half-heartedly through the various vegetables which grew in plots around them. Adrian and Mike followed the stream until they reached the tunnel which went under the dual carriageway that ran past the allotment. The tunnel was heavy with vegetation and the stream was barely visible. "Come on," said Mike, "She won't be in there, she can't swim."

"I will go in and have a look though, you never know, we have to check everywhere." Adrian replied. He stepped down the shallow bank into the stream and made his way through the vegetation into the tunnel itself.

Mike, who was still of the mind-set that Savannah was alive and hiding in a friend's house somewhere stood and waited for Adrian to return. He exchanged pleasantries with the cameraman who had followed him and confirmed with them his belief of where and how they would find Savannah.

"Oh my fucking god," a cry came from inside the tunnel.

The cameraman immediately put his mobile video recorder up to his eye and pointed it in the direction of the tunnel where he had heard Adrian make that comment.

Mike and the cameraman heard the sounds of footsteps splashing in the stream and watched Adrian come out of the tunnel, carrying the grey and swollen body of a child in his arms; laid flat on its back with legs and arms dangling towards the ground. Long brown hair hung over the child's eyes obscuring its face.

Mike stepped forwards and moved the hair out of the way.

"It's her." he shouted. "It's Savannah, oh my God." He sank to the floor on his knees and began to cry.

The cameraman propped his camera in the crook of his arm and reached for his mobile phone. He rang the number on the leaflet after calling his reporter colleague. PC Mann answered and he said, "We've found her, she's dead. You need to come to the stream behind the allotment, now."

Adrian stepped out of the river and sat down on the grass, cradling Savannah in his arms. He waited for the police to arrive so he could deliver his angel into their arms.

Jocasta heard amongst her group that Savannah's dead body had been found. When she was told that it was at the allotment, her first thought was of Adrian as she knew he had been in the group which had gone to that area to conduct the search. Rather than return to the Community Centre as asked, Jocasta made her way to the allotment. She had to be sure that Adrian was ok.

When she arrived at the allotment it was teeming with police officers, men in white suits, cameramen and reporters. Countless vehicles were parked in the alleyway leading up to the gates and Jocasta carefully moved herself around them until she got to the rusted gates at the end of the alleyway. She was stopped by a young officer as she tried to go through them.

"I'm sorry Ma'am, you can't go in there," said the officer.

"My son was on the search party." Jocasta told him. "Please I have to see if he's ok."

"Ma'am I can't let you in there, we have a job to do and we don't want to contaminate the scene any more than is necessary. Let me find out where your son's gone, what's his name?"

"Adrian Brown."

The officer got onto his radio and quietly spoke into the receiver. He twiddled the knobs on the radio and then held it close to his ear, the crowds about him making it difficult for him to hear. After a brief conversation the officer turned back to Jocasta and said, "It seems as if it was your son who found her ma'am."

Jocasta gasped, she was shocked; poor Adrian, she thought, to have seen a dead body, he must be in a really bad way. "Well I really must go to him then, where is he now?" she asked.

"He's been taken back to Olinsbury police station so that he can make a statement. If you want to see him you will need to go there. Now please ma'am, you really do need to leave the scene."

"Yes ok, thank you." Jocasta turned away from the officer and tried to work out her best course of action. The only way she could think of getting to Adrian was by bus so she made her way back towards her estate and waited twenty minutes for a bus to come along. As she sat on the bus all she could think about was how Adrian must be feeling. She had never seen a dead body before, she could only imagine what that must be like and to see a dead child must be ten times worse in her estimation. She was concerned that this may psychologically affect Adrian and resolved to take him to the GP when they were able so she could get him some counselling. She wasn't going to let this spoil Adrian's life.

Jocasta was so consumed in her worry for Adrian, she barely gave little Savannah a thought. Not being directly related to her, Jocasta did not feel affected by Savannah's death. It was no different to how she felt when children were reported in the media. She was sad and found it despicable, yes, but it only warranted a thought when actually pushed in her face by the papers or the television. Her feelings about it disintegrated along with the newspapers the news was written on. This time, however, something had happened to her son and she was desperately worried about how he might be suffering.

Jocasta arrived at the police station and went straight to the front counter to ask after Adrian. A man in a grey suit came out of a door leading off the reception area and made his way towards her.

"Hello ma'am, I'm the investigating officer in this case, my name is Detective Inspector Turnbull." He held out his hand to shake Jocasta's and she obliged. She looked up and thought what a handsome man he was. Certainly a man who could turn her mind away from a situation - if only briefly - he was a silver fox just like Philip Schofield she thought. To add to this, he was tanned and had laughter lines around his eyes, the thing she noticed most about him though were the green eyes which gazed upon her. She had seen most colour eyes but none so vividly green as these, they looked as if they could see into her very soul. DI Turnbull gave a slight cough alerting Jocasta to the fact she still had hold of his hand and had been shaking it for longer than was required. She pulled her hand away.

"Are you Mrs Brown?" He enquired.

"It's Miss Brown. Where's my son?"

"He's just giving his statement to police and we need to take his fingerprints and DNA for elimination purposes." He told her.

Jocasta didn't understand what DI Turnbull was saying. "What does that mean?" she asked.

DI Turnbull cleared his throat and explained. "Your son found Savannah, Miss Brown. He picked her up from the stream and carried her to the bank. He may well have left his fingerprints or DNA at the scene or on Savannah so we need to identify them in the hope we can separate them from anything her killer may have left."

"Was she murdered then?" Jocasta was horrified by this notion. She had believed that maybe Savannah had fallen in the stream and banged her head, that it had been accidental. It hadn't occurred to her that Savannah may have been brutally murdered.

"It looks that way." DI Turnbull started to shift from one foot to another, he obviously had some place else he wanted to be. "I can't really discuss it any further with you, if you would like to take a seat we will send Adrian out to you when he's ready."

"OK thanks." Jocasta sat in the same blue seat she had sat in six years ago, the last time Adrian was at the station. She sat back and watched the continuous stream of humanity which came and went from the police station. She was glad that at least this time Adrian was here because he was a hero rather than a villain. Knowing there was no way she would get to watch Eastenders now; Jocasta sat back and closed her eyes to wait for her son, her hero, her Adrian.

Chapter 16

'Keep your love for each other at full strength because love covers a multitude of sins.'
    I Peter 4:8

Detective Inspector Todd Turnbull was known as Todger to his friends and colleagues, mainly because he had been rumoured to be 'over the side' with nearly every female police officer he had ever met. Having such a reputation within the police did not make Todd an outcast amongst his colleagues. He was a good copper, had earned his right to be an inspector and was respected as a good detective who hadn't lost sight of his job, despite being promoted into an office. He was known as someone who got his hands dirty and actively participated in investigations rather than just overseeing them from behind a desk. Todd actually believed it was an advantage to gain a nickname amongst his peers, even though he hadn't earned that particular accolade. In reality he had only slept with ten women; which at the age of forty was not that many. His handsome looks made him the pursued rather than the pursuer and the females never seemed to brag about the fact he'd knocked *them* back.

When the report landed on his desk about Savannah West's disappearance he was of the same opinion that she was just another runaway teen. It came as a shock to him when a call came from PC Mann informing him the little girl had been found in a stream that morning. To Todd's chagrin the body had been moved and touched by a few people before proper police protocol could be put into place to preserve the crime scene. Todd was annoyed that appropriate steps hadn't been taken to ensure the people searching knew not to touch anything they found, but he understood that no one really expected to find anything.

He had arrived at the allotments to find the little girl lying naked on the grass by the stream. She didn't seem like a human being, her skin was no longer the colour of flesh, she was grey and swollen a gaping wound was evident on her chest. Her eyes were half open, it was as if she was looking directly at him, waiting for him to speak to her, but he knew the eyes saw nothing and never would again. Todd found himself drawn to her, he had an urge to pick her up and hold her. She was so young, he needed to cuddle and protect her. Todd fought these urges and forced himself to turn away from Savannah. He looked for the Scenes of Crime officer who was usually covered head to toe in white protective overalls. He saw her now coming out from the tunnel the stream flowed into.

"Jan." he shouted, getting her attention.

"Jan, come over here." He gestured at her to leave the stream and join him on the bank. Jan came over, only her chubby face visible in the elasticated surround of her paper hood.

"Hello sir." Jan came to stand beside him.

"What have you found?" Todd asked her.

"Well there's nowhere to get fingerprints from Guv." She shrugged. "She was found in running water; anything that may have been there has probably been washed away. Hopefully we can get something from her body. Poor little mite."

Todd returned his gaze to Savannah, he couldn't stand to see her so bare against the ground.

"Ok do we actually need her here still?" he shouted at the people milling around. They all stopped to listen to their Inspector.

"Has the photographer finished?" Todd asked.

"Yes Guv." The photographer waved his camera at Todd.

"Has the Coroner carried out his investigations?"

"Yes Guv," came the group response.

"Right then get her covered up and get the ambulance men to pick her up and take her to the Coroner's office. If you had finished you should have covered her up, she's a baby for fucks sake." Todd knew they had probably left Savannah's corpse in situ so he, as the investigating officer, could see her. But as it was not the actual spot she had died in, he saw no purpose in that. He turned to his DS who had walked up beside him.

"OK Mary, get the search team in here. I need these allotments gone over with a fine toothcomb. I want to know if this is where she died, we need to find her clothes and we need to know how she got in that tunnel."

"Yes Guv."

"Where is the person who found her?"

DS Mary Webb gestured to Adrian and Mike who were at the edge of the allotment; Mike still on the ground, his grief apparently taking away his ability to stand. Adrian was just looking in their direction, wet up to the knees, hands in pockets, watching the goings on around him.

"The one standing up found her sir," said DS Webb. "The one on the floor is her step-dad."

"Her step-dad; what, he was here when she was found?" asked Todd.

"Yes he was on the search party that came to the allotments."

"That's convenient." Todd was already looking for suspects. A study of child killers he had read suggested the killer would often return to a crime scene and would even take some part in the investigation. It was reported that most killers who had been caught had been spoken to in the first week of investigation. Todd knew all of this and also knew that it was often somebody known to the victim. Right now Mike the stepfather was looking to be his most likely candidate for investigation.

Todd once again encouraged his staff to be thorough and to remove Savannah's body as quickly as possible. He wanted her looked at in the confines of the mortuary so they could get as much evidence as possible and catch the daemon who had killed this poor child. He demanded that the stepfather and the boy who had found the body, be taken to the police station so they could be questioned and then decided to head back there also as he wanted to prepare the questions to ask Savannah's stepfather. Hopefully the right question with the right delivery would get Todd the answers he needed.

As Todd went to leave the allotment he heard a heart wrenching screech come from the entrance.

"My baby, my baby, oh my baby." came the cry. He saw a woman stumble through the gates and down on the ground beside the stepfather. The woman started hitting the man about the head and shoulders and he sat, allowing the blows to rain down upon him. A police officer stepped in and grabbed the woman under her arms, pulling her up into his embrace where she then relented and stood crying into the officer's shoulder.

"The mother," DS Webb said.

"Yeah thanks Mary, I'd worked that one out for myself." sniffed Todd. "She doesn't seem too happy with her fella does she?"

DS Webb shrugged, "Wouldn't surprise me if she thinks he did it." She said.

"You know, I was just thinking the same thing." Todd confided in her, "What a fucked up world we live in."

* * *

Will Turner, the Coroner; finished his autopsy

of Savannah West. Having been a Coroner for many years he had seen copious amounts of dead bodies in differing degrees of decay. Nothing turned his stomach; he could quite easily eat his lunch whilst peering at the remains of an elderly man who had not been discovered until after the build-up of his stomach acid had caused him to explode.

Recently however, Will had become a father to a beautiful baby girl called Betsy-Lou. She was the most precious thing he had ever set eyes on and a great desire to protect her had overcome him. Whilst he may never grow up enough to stop playing with his remote controlled planes, he had certainly matured into a nurturing father who understood the love a parent has for their child. Savannah's autopsy was his first child's body since his life changing fatherhood and he found himself more and more enraged as he uncovered the circumstances of her death.

DI Turnbull entered the room once the autopsy was complete. He never entered whilst a body was on the table. He didn't feel the need to share in every grisly detail of a victim's dissection and Todd felt it was more respectful to give them their privacy, even in death.

"Hi Will, what have you got for me, and please;" He held up his hand before Will could reply. "No medical jargon, just give it to me straight."

"OK," Will readied himself to deliver the news, "I'm afraid she was raped and sodomised."

Todd took a step back to lean on the bench near the wall of the sterile environment. He had been expecting rape or some sort of sexual abuse but had not expected such complete violation of a young girl.

"Are you ok?" asked Will.

"Yes, yes, poor little thing, carry on Will, sorry; are there any evidential fluids?"

"No semen; he either wore a condom or didn't ejaculate. We've taken some samples of her cells and we can see if there's any DNA that may have been left behind, but doesn't look hopeful." Will Turner went on to explain that Savannah had been raped and her throat had been crushed causing her death. It was believed post-mortem that the assailant had then sodomised Savannah and she had been bitten savagely on her left breast. When Todd asked Will how he knew those things had happened post mortem, Will explained that the bite was so deep they would have caused heavy blood loss had the heart still been pumping.

"Any chance of getting impressions of the bite marks?" Todd enquired; he knew that dental records could help him to match the bite marks to the teeth of the biter.

"No chance at all." Will told him, "The bite was ragged; it's as if the person bit and then twisted with their teeth. There are no clear teeth marks at all. Add to that she's been got at by rats..."

"Please, stop, I get it."

Todd felt physically sick at the thought that not only had someone raped and killed Savannah but they had continued to defile her when she no longer breathed. She was dead, unresponsive and had still been used like a toy. He was ready to question the stepfather; it was time to bring him to justice.

* * *

"Right Mr Scammell, let me first start by saying I am very sorry for your loss."

"I should be with her mother, I should be with Mae." Mike Scammell looked like a broken man. Years of heroin and alcohol abuse had not been kind to him. His eyes were droopy like a hound dog and tears dripped from them intermittently. Rubbing his stubbly, scar infested face, Mike looked up at Todd.

"I shouldn't be here, she needs me." He stated.

"Mr Scammell, Mike, we will try to get you home as quickly as possible but as you were there when she was found..."

"Savannah. Her name is Savannah; not 'she.'" Mike snapped. "Say her name, Savannah." He tapped the table with a dirty finger. "Savannah West, my daughter." He raised his voice. "I may not be the best stepdad but I'm the only one she's got... had." He muttered before weeping into his hands.

"Sorry Mike. It must be a very hard time for you." Todd was surprised at how this interview was going. A suspicion of guilt had made him believe Mike would be calm and collected, careful in his responses and probably mostly irresponsive in case he said something he shouldn't. Mike's passionate replies and obvious emotion made Todd begin to believe Mike may be innocent of any wrongdoing. Todd had been fooled before, however, so knew not to trust his own instincts completely but to let the evidence do the talking.

"We just need to ask you a few things so we can be sure we help Savannah and find the person who did this to her. Mike?"

"Yes."

"We just want to know what happened today." Todd sat back and waited to hear Mike's story.

Mike Scammell gave Todd an account of the day's happenings. How the groups had met and gone out searching.

"I was talking to that young lad and we went over to the stream. I didn't think she would be in *there*." Mike gulped and fresh tears began to flow. "But he just walked out with her in his fucking arms; just like that." He clicked his fingers. "There she was... dead. Oh my God. Dead, she was dead; so fucking dead." Mike began to rock in his chair, cuddling his body with his arms. Todd reached out to him and patted his arm.

"Mike, I'm sorry to have to ask you this but can you tell me what you were doing on New Year's Eve." Todd waited for the onslaught that was surely to come when Mike realised the implications of what Todd was asking.

"Oh my God, no, no, no." Mike moaned, rocking continuously backwards and forwards.

"We have to ask Mike, it's very important that we know where everyone was." Todd reassured him. Mike paused to compose himself, then rubbed his hands down his face, wiping away snot and tears in one swoop, took a deep breath and began to speak.

"Me and Mae were having a row, we'd both been drinking, I'd been on the heroin and we starting rowing."

"What was the argument about?" Todd asked.

"I don't know; something stupid." Mike shook his head, "Anyway it got loud and I smashed the house up, Mae was screaming and doing my fucking head in, I just had to get out of there."

"Where were the children Mike? Where were Savannah and Andrew?" Todd urged him.

"They were... I don't know, in the bedroom I suppose. They always get out of the way when we argue."

"Did you see them in the bedroom?"

"What? No, I wasn't looking for them, I didn't care about them, I had the hump for fucks sake. I was pissed and stoned and she was bending my ear."

"Ok, carry on, what happened next?"

"Well I just left. I walked out and went to some crack house in Olinsbury." Mike rubbed his face again. "Stayed there for the night and then went home with my tail between my legs the next day as I always do."

"Ok Mike, where was the crack house?" Todd asked.

"You're joking mate, I aint telling you that." Mike laughed. "I'll get fucking killed. It's more than my life is worth."

"Any way we can prove what you're saying Mike? It's important." Todd told him.

"I don't know, there were some other crack heads there, do you know Stupid Billy?"

"The kid that hangs around Barton's Corner?" Todd knew Stupid Billy well; he was a notorious crack head who occasionally hung around a shopping centre in Olinsbury.

"Yeah that's him," confirmed Mike. "He saw me, he can tell you I was there."

Todd pointed out to Mike that alibis from junkies were hardly reliable, but said he would look into them. He had no choice but to bail Mike from the station; suspicion was not enough to keep him locked up. Todd was going to have to find the often elusive Stupid Billy, so he could check Mike's alibi and either prove or disprove what he had said. It appeared to Todd anyhow that Mike was not looking so likely for the killing of Savannah; he just seemed too passionate about her death. The gut instinct which Todd had had initially was now gone.

Todd knew that he also had to check out any other statements that had been made and to go over the background of any parties concerned. Feeling frustrated that he was getting nowhere with the step-father, he spent some time looking at the mother, Mae. Rather unusually there were no Social Services reports for the family. It seemed as if Mae West and her two children lived uneventful lives. He had heard rumour that Mae was an alcoholic, but this did not seem to have had any detrimental effect on the family as Social Services had never had cause to step in and take control of the care of the children. Mae stated she had been home all night on New Year's Eve and had fallen asleep after the row she had had with Mike. There was nobody other than her eight year old son Andrew to verify her story, but considering Savannah had been so brutally violated, it was clear to Todd that she was not responsible and he couldn't bring himself to believe that Mae knew who had assaulted Savannah or that she may have been party to it; even considering a woman bearing the same name had done just that in the past. The case of Fred and Rose West came to his mind, reinforcing that anything was possible so Todd kept Mae on his suspect list just in case.

The only other person Todd had on his list currently was the person who had found Savannah, Adrian Brown. He was a young lad who lived with his mother around the corner from Savannah. Reports showed that Adrian, who worked in the local Big Value, had volunteered to join in the hunt and had been the one to actually find Savannah's body; carrying her out of the tunnel and into the view of the cameraman who had now made his fortune, selling that very footage to every News channel across the world.

Todd called up Adrian's background on the Police National Computer as it was standard procedure for him to check out everything in cases involving sexual contact with children. He found the report from PC Judd in October 2003 where Adrian had been arrested for sexually assaulting a young girl at his school. Although the case had not been proceeded with, PC Judd had written his opinion in the conclusion of his report. Todd read this now.

'It is my opinion that Adrian Brown is guilty of the sexual assault on Charmaine Sprint. Unfortunately Charmaine suffers from Asperger's Syndrome and was unable to provide police with a statement which would give enough evidence to prove his guilt. The Crown Prosecution Service lawyer decided it was not in the public interest to proceed with a prosecution.'

Todd knew this was a typical occurrence in matters of sexual contact. It was a matter of one word against the other and the victims needed to be very certain of what they were saying and able to stand up to the questioning from a defence barrister who would try their very hardest to discredit them. It was sad but true. Todd could understand why this case had never gone anywhere but thanks to the information being kept he now had a seed of suspicion planted into his inquisitive mind.

How much of a coincidence was it that the person who finds the dead child had previously come to police attention for a sexual assault?

Bearing in mind what he knew about offenders returning to the scene and liking to make contact with the investigation, Todd now realised that Adrian was just as likely a suspect as the stepfather. He decided he would go and visit Adrian Brown and find out just what *he* was up to on New Year's Eve.

* * *

Mother Be The Judge

Detective Inspector Todd Turnbull announced his arrival to the customer service desk at Big Value. The female customer service operative's face went from bored to interested in the glimpse of an eye and she was using her best professional persona to assist him. Todd told her he was looking for Adrian Brown and she came out from her desk to direct him to where Adrian was working. Todd was led to the refrigerated store room situated just off the drinks aisle of the store. He followed the service operative's feet as they click clacked their way along the shiny shop floor.

"Adrian, this is Detective Inspector Turnbull, he wants to talk to you." She said into the air around her. A dark haired youth stepped out from the numerous stacks of boxes and stood in front of Todd.

"Thank you very much; I need to speak to Mr Brown in private if that's ok with you?" Todd gave the woman one of his winning smiles and she swooned her way back out of the refrigerated room.

Todd turned to the lad in front of him. He noted that Adrian was not a good looking lad; buck teeth, black fuzzy hair and a big hairy caterpillar stuck above his eyes. Todd felt sorry for him although he envied the peace this must bring the lad. It was quite draining being constantly pursued by women and men alike.

"You are the one who found Savannah West, is that right?" Todd decided to get straight to business; he didn't want to give the lad a chance to think of an answer to his questions.

"Yeah," Adrian replied.

"Ok, I just need to ask you what you were doing

on New Year's Eve, between about 9pm and 8am the following morning?" This was the time span Will Turner had given Todd for time of death. The cold and damp had made it more difficult to establish a smaller window of time as cold always slowed the onset of decomposition.

"I was at home." Adrian turned away from Todd and began opening a box on top of one of the stacks. "Why?" he seemed nonchalant, but Todd knew this was often a ruse to hide guilt.

"Well we believe that's the timeframe Savannah may have died in."

"What does that have to do with me?" asked Adrian, "I didn't kill her."

"I'm not saying you did." Appeased Todd, "It's standard procedure to ask these questions of everyone close to the investigation.

"Oh." Adrian shrugged. "Well as I said, I was at home all night."

"Did you go out at all?"

"No."

"Is there anyone who can verify that?" asked Todd.

"My mother, we had a drink, it was New Year's Eve." Adrian continued to open his boxes and remove various cold food items; stacking them on a portable trolley ready to be put out on sale.

"How well did you know Savannah, Adrian?"

Adrian stopped what he was doing and pulled a face which made him seem as though he was considering the question. "What do you mean how well?" Adrian asked.

"Well did you know her to talk to or did you just know her from around the estate?" Todd didn't believe he had asked a difficult question; Adrian still seemed to be contemplating his answer which annoyed Todd.

"Did you know her name?" He asked, deciding he would have to ask leading questions to get the information he wanted.

"Yes."

"Did you ever talk to her?"

"No."

"Never? She only lived around the corner; did she play in the park outside your house?"

"Yeah but she's not my friend. She's only eleven. I'm eighteen, it's not like we would bother talking to each other is it?" said Adrian. He returned once again to unpacking boxes.

* * *

Todd could think of nothing else to ask Adrian at this point so said goodbye and made his way around to Adrian's flat. Not happy with the answers Adrian had given him and still suspicious he may be involved, Todd decided to check on Adrian's story about being at home, with his mother.

He knocked on the front door and it was opened after a short while. Todd once again met the woman who had shaken his hand for an uncomfortably long time at the police station. She was just as ugly as her son, with the same caterpillar eyebrow. He could see why Adrian was so unfortunate in the looks department.

Jocasta looked at DI Turnbull and once again marvelled at how handsome he was. "Hello?" she said.

"Hi, Mrs Brown?"

"It's Miss." Jocasta could feel herself blushing when she said this, realising she wanted to correct him so he knew she was single and available instead of her usual pride at being a single parent.

"Miss Brown, sorry, may I come in?" I just have a few questions about your son."

"Adrian? Why, what has happened? Is he ok?"

"Nothing has happened to Adrian." Todd was confounded that this woman had not made a connection to the police, Adrian and little Savannah. Had she not been aware of the investigation going on, on her very doorstep?

"Adrian found Savannah Miss Brown, he is connected to the investigation and we have to ask the same questions of everyone involved."

"Oh, ok." Jocasta gestured for Todd to come into the hallway and shut the front door. She stood and waited for the questions Todd had to ask her.

"Can you tell me where Adrian was on New Year's Eve?" Todd asked her.

"Oh he was home with me; we were watching the countdown to New Year's and drinking wine. We even sang Auld Lang Syne." She smiled as she remembered.

"And what about New Year's Day, the morning, in particular between midnight and 8 o'clock; can you tell me where he was then?" asked Todd.

Jocasta suddenly had a flashback, the memories of that New Year's morning playing in slow motion in her brain; the sound of the door waking her from her sleep. Adrian coming into the house, his legs wet up to the knee; Adrian, heading straight for the shower and Adrian, washing his clothes; totally out of character. She then flashed back to Adrian touching Savannah's photo on the television screen and Adrian deleting unknown pages from his computer.

"He went to bed about 1 o'clock and then got up about 7ish for his breakfast." She said. "I made him a ham omelette; he likes ham omelettes, especially with mushrooms." She was aware she was wittering but Jocasta carried on until the officer stopped her.

"OK Miss Brown, I understand. Can you be sure he didn't leave the flat?"

"Oh yes, I double lock the door at night. It's very loud and I'm a very light sleeper. I would know if he left the flat."

Todd sighed, he was sure he had been onto something and whilst it was not unheard of for parents to provide their children with false alibis, he had nothing to refute it, so would have to accept it for now. The frustrating thing here was Todd couldn't use any DNA or fingerprint evidence as Adrian had a reasonable explanation for his to be on Savannah's body. Todd said his goodbyes to Jocasta and left for the Coroner's office in the hope Adrian's DNA may be discovered in the samples taken from inside Savannah rather than just on the outside of her body.

* * *

Jocasta shut the door behind the Inspector as he left. She turned her back to the door and leant on it. The flashbacks she had just had, replayed themselves over and over in her head. Was it possible that Adrian, good, sweet and loving Adrian could have been involved in the rape and murder of a young girl?

Jocasta was not a stupid person. She was just a woman who was blinded by her love for her only child. From the day he was born it was her life's ambition to protect Adrian from everything and she had done that unquestioningly in every circumstance Adrian had got himself into. The veil of darkness which came with denial now began to remove itself from her eyes and heart as she realised that two of those circumstances consisted of allegations against Adrian, suggesting he had touched young girls. Jocasta realised that she had just protected Adrian once again from arrest by the police. It was dawning on her now that there was a very definite possibility that Adrian was in some way responsible for the demise of Savannah. Constant images of his wet legs reminded her Savannah was found in a stream. The connection was undeniable.

"Oh... my... god." She said and sank to her knees, imagining what the child must have been thinking

Mother Be The Judge

when she was raped and how her little face must have been in a rictus of pain and fear. Jocasta felt nausea overcome her; she ran to the toilet and purged her stomach contents into the gleaming white bowl, dirtying the sides of the toilet just as the image of her son committing such a foul act dirtied her imagination.

Jocasta heard the front door open and Adrian come into the flat. She flushed the toilet and went out to meet him, intending on asking him what part he had played in the death of Savannah.

As they met in the corridor the words died in her mouth. She looked at Adrian's beautiful innocent face. At his blue eyes and dark hair and just couldn't believe him possible of such vile acts.

"Hi mum." Adrian smiled at her. "Did the police come and see you? They asked me some weird questions. I think they think I had something to do with it. Can you believe that?" he watched her closely for her reaction.

Jocasta considered Adrian for a short while and then smiled back. "No." She said. "I can't believe it. I told that officer you were here all night and all morning. You can't possibly have hurt that poor girl."

"Exactly," he said, "Thanks mum." He pecked her on the cheek and made towards his bedroom. "What's for tea?"

"Shepherd's pie," Jocasta smiled at him.

"Oh my favourite," Adrian said with glee.

Jocasta chided herself for ever thinking Adrian could be responsible for murder of all things. She pushed the images to the back of her mind and shut the door on any suspicion she <u>may have had</u>; the veil of denial coming back thick and fast. The police were just looking for a scape goat because they could not do their jobs properly and find the killer. Once again Jocasta felt she had done the right thing in protecting her son from bullies.

Book 3

Chapter 17

'The soul that has conceived one wickedness can nurse no good thereafter.'
Sophocles

March 2012

The media coverage on Savannah's death went from being daily to just a quick mention once a week until finally, four months later, no News coverage at all. Crimewatch played a reconstruction on the first anniversary asking for any witnesses to come forward, but to no avail. It seemed as if Savannah's assailant would never be brought to justice.

Jocasta continued to spend her days looking after Adrian and each day that passed made her more certain of his innocence. Soon the whole scenario was just a distant memory and no one but Savannah's parents gave that dead little girl another thought.

* * *

Adrian had been very careful to never mention Savannah either at work or at home. It seemed to him his genius at 'finding' Savannah had saved him from discovery. When the police inspector had come asking questions at his place of work, Adrian had almost lost his nerve; he had congratulated himself on his fine acting and was pleased to find his mother had provided him with a cast iron alibi. Either she had forgotten about his early morning return or was so blinded by her love for him that she had lied to protect him. Adrian hadn't cared which it was, although he suspected the latter was the most likely scenario.

Although Adrian had gotten away with his indiscretion with Savannah, he hadn't wanted to immediately repeat the event. He had taken Savannah's knickers as a token to remind him of the loss of his virginity to such an angel and had been content to replay their night together in his head whenever he felt any sexual urges. Adrian knew that to kill another girl again without careful planning would almost certainly get him caught and consign him to a long life behind bars; he intended to avoid that and believed he was clever enough to do so.

Lacey had never returned to the Fern Bridge. Adrian hadn't known the reasons behind it until his mother told him she had heard the local gossips discussing Lacey and her situation. Apparently Lacey's mother had drunk away the housing benefit each week rather than pay the rent and the whole family had been evicted. Lacey and Co were now living in a small town in Yorkshire. Adrian was saddened he had never got a chance to taste the delights Lacey may have had to offer; he wondered if she ever thought of him but supposed she was busy showing her fanny to some other boy by now.

Time had gone on and Adrian spent more and more time looking at the girls playing in the park outside his window. He had set up a cheap camera and would take a quick picture if ever a skirt blew up or a girl would pull a face he liked the look of. Adrian would also visit Riddles Park off Twockford Road, near to his estate. Elisworth Recreation Centre backed onto the park and had very large windows allowing natural light to get into the pool room. If Adrian stood in the right part of the bushes he could happily watch the young girls swimming in the pool in their skimpy costumes and even bikinis, if he was lucky. Adrian had contented himself like this for the last two years, opting for pornography, voyeurism and self-re-enactment rather than the actual physical act. He was getting frustrated, however; the memories of Savannah were dull in his mind. He couldn't quite remember the feel of her skin or the juiciness of her as he bit into her sweet flesh. Adrian believed he had waited long enough; it was time for him to make another angel.

* * *

Having a sexual touching allegation on his record made it very difficult for Adrian to find a situation where he could meet a girl. He wanted to have a relationship with his new angel. To have a connection with her like he had with Lacey. Adrian still believed that if he had had love for someone it would make the killing all the sweeter and would help him achieve the release he was yet to experience. He had tried Scouts, Sea Cadets, Football Coach, Youth Club Assistant, but had been blocked each time by a request for a police background check. After the first time he agreed to do this had resulted in the Charmaine incident being relayed to the interested party, he never bothered to agree again, but considered there may be an organisation trusting enough not to bother with the police check. Annoyingly he was yet to find any group willing to blindly accept him; he cursed the 'do gooders' who spent all their time sticking their noses into everyone's business. Adrian had to content himself with visiting the library. It was a place where parents sent their children regularly to read alone. As it was attached to the swimming pool, Adrian would often find himself surrounded by unattended children, left by their parents whilst they tended to brothers and sisters who were attending their relative lessons.

Also sent to the library were the 'Homework Club' as Adrian like to refer to them; young girls and boys who would visit the library after school to do their homework and wait for the time their parents would be home from work and the house would be available to them once again.

Most of these children were either too young or too old for Adrian's taste. He liked girls who were on the brink of womanhood, old enough to converse with but not so old they would have all the undesirable bumps and hair like his mother. The girls often went to the library in groups or in pairs so Adrian was

Mother Be The Judge

unable to approach them. He waited patiently each time he visited, sitting in his regular chair which was near to the study tables. Adrian believed that if he was patient enough his angel would eventually come. He also enjoyed the solitude away from his pig of a mother who seemed ever more determined to treat him like a twelve year old, constantly asking him where he was going and checking he was at work when he said he would be. He had never bought a mobile phone, one, because he didn't actually have anyone other than work to speak to and two, so his mother couldn't keep up her constant surveillance of him. Adrian had excluded his mother from his bedroom, telling her he preferred to tidy it himself. He also banned her from the library with a threat of desertion should she ever step foot in his safe haven.

Adrian sat now in his chair in the library. He was holding a book he had found called American Psycho; it was a truly depraved book where a man took women back to his apartment, nailed them to the floor and dismembered them for pleasure. Adrian liked reading the book; it gave him a funny feeling in his stomach when he read it. He actually had his own copy at home which was dog eared where he had read it so much, but he wasn't reading it now; now it was just a prop in his library façade.

A young girl came and sat at the study tables in the library. She had long ginger hair in a very thick plait hanging down to her waist. The girl wore thick lensed glasses in pink Dolce and Gabbana frames, an attempt Adrian thought, at making the glasses cool. It wasn't possible to know how big her eyes were as the lenses had such a magnifying effect on her blue eyes, they appeared to bulge out of her head. To add to the poor girls unfortunate appearance, she had top and bottom railway track braces which caused her lips to hang open constantly. Adrian even saw dribble occasionally escape from the freckled face.

It was no surprise to Adrian that this girl came alone to the library; he remembered how he was outcast by his own classmates for not conforming to their idea of handsome. He knew it was very probable this girl was subjected to daily bullying which would not dissipate on returning home thanks to the internet being the perfect conduit for cyber bullies to continue their relentless campaign to mercilessly pester and persecute their victims.

Adrian felt fate had been good to him. His patience and persistence had rewarded him with the perfect candidate for the type of love he had to offer. He had seen her now on three other occasions, Wednesday afternoons seemed to be the time she would come and sit on the table, books in front of her, but eyes not seeing the text as she sat and pondered her miserable existence. On the last occasion her eyes had flickered briefly in Adrian's direction and he had given her a shy smile before returning his gaze to his book. This week Adrian watched as the girl took out her books and pencil case, carefully removing pens, pencils and ruler and lining them up on the table in front of her. Her chin crinkled and a fat tear escaped from under her glasses making its way slowly to her open mouth. Adrian took this as his queue to make first contact with his new angel.

He didn't need to get up from his chair or raise his voice as the girl sat at the nearest table to him, so he just said in his normal voice, "Are you alright?"

The girl nodded her head and gave a small smile then took off her glasses to wipe her now tiny eyes.

"Yes I'm ok." She said.

"You don't look ok." Adrian said, "What is it? Are you being bullied?"

The girl was shocked that Adrian had been spot on. Her parents were oblivious to the bullying, choosing instead to shrug it off as childhood antics, just telling her to, "Laugh with them," and suggesting the bullies would, "Soon get bored."

"How did you know?" she asked Adrian.

"I've been there." He gestured to the chair she sat on. "Used to come here all the time when I was being bullied." He gave a short laugh. "I still come here."

The girl smiled again and then put her glasses back on, restoring her eyes to their magnified size. She looked once again at the text book in front of her.

"What's your name?" Adrian asked her.

"Tiffany." She said.

"That's a lovely name."

"Not when people call you Tit Fanny it isn't." Tiffany smiled waiting for Adrian to smile with her. He smiled back and they continued to sit in companionable silence for the next few minutes.

"I'm Adrian." He said, "I'm always here."

"Yeah I know I've seen you here before."

"Yeah, part of the furniture I am." He grinned, "I don't even like reading. It's just a place to sit."

"Same here," said Tiffany. "I've already done my homework."

The two of them sat for another hour, exchanging pleasantries; Adrian responding to all Tiffany's little jokes and sympathising with her situation, giving her his own bullying analogies. Eventually Tiffany made her excuses and made to leave. Her parents would be home at 5:30 and she had to be in, in time for tea.

"When are you coming again?" asked Adrian.

"I might come tomorrow." Said Tiffany, she was pleased to have somebody who understood what she was going through. He wasn't very nice to look at but he was really nice to talk to and that's all she wanted.

"OK well see you tomorrow then?" asked Adrian.

"Yeah, see you tomorrow." Tiffany waved good-bye and left the library.

Adrian was thrilled with this meeting. Tiffany was perfect for him; she was old enough to not have that childish way of speaking that Adrian could not cope with but young enough to have not reached puberty. Adrian guessed she must be eleven or twelve years old. He left the library and went home to retrieve Savannah's knickers so he could spend some time reliving their special moment. He would have to leave Savannah behind now as another angel had entered his life.

* * *

The next day Adrian went to work at 6am and spent the morning cleaning shelves and restocking them. He was getting sick of his job, it had never served its purpose of getting him closer to girls but it did at least get him out of the house. Considering he had worked there now for three years, he thought there should have been a few opportunities at least, but he had never made it onto the tills and spent most of his time opening boxes in the refrigerated store room. He hadn't even made any friends and it wasn't because of his looks; half of Big Value was inhabited by people just as facially challenged as Adrian. The reason he could not get on with them was because they were so *different* to him. Adrian had no need to use his talent of manipulation on them because it would serve him no purpose. The manager who had originally employed him had moved on to a bigger store and Adrian had been left with a female manager in her fifties who seemed untouched by Adrian's greatness. He had tried several times to convince her he would be better off on the tills or customer service, only to be brushed off with, "But you do such a good job with the sausage display." Adrian often envisioned shoving those sausages in all of the woman's orifices until she was just one fat sausage herself. All the other staff had their own cliques and unless Adrian was going to become Mr Popular overnight, he was never going to be in any of them. All in all he continued his job at Big Value, pretty much ignored and left to get on with things. Adrian didn't mind, Big Value was just a few hours a day. His real life started when he returned home to his computer and went into chat rooms.

He would trawl the chat rooms for opportunities to talk to young girls, often pretending to be a girl himself. In this way he would learn about how girls thought, what their feelings were and what worried them. Online Adrian had hundreds of friends; he had a Facebook page in the name of Gracie Smith with a profile photo of a pretty thirteen year old he had found in a picture book printed in the 1970's. He had cropped the picture and pasted it in, then began to request friends. He would request anyone on there who had a young picture. It wasn't possible to know their ages as Facebook had a rule of over thirteen's only. Adrian was always surprised when someone accepted him; people were so trusting online and the youngsters just seemed to want to get as many friends as possible so they looked the most popular on there. The only downside to this activity was that he was pretending to be a girl so although he was able to view their pictures and comment or chat with the girls; this could never lead to a meeting or a relationship. Adrian just had to content himself with his imagination, but at least he had a different girl to imagine every night.

Another pastime for Adrian online was networking with other like-minded souls. If he found the right website by typing in trigger words like, 'young girl' 'school girl sucks' etc. he could open up a whole network of men *and* women who enjoyed the same passion as Adrian. He had discovered sites where he could download movies of girls, just his type, performing sexual acts and not always willingly. Adrian particularly like the more barbaric movies where sex was forced and brutal; snuff movies were high on Adrian's agenda of something to watch but these were very difficult to come across, even online. Adrian had to content himself with his own homemade snuff movie which played often, over and over in his head. He made a decision that should the opportunity ever arise again he would make sure he had a video camera so he could capture the moment when his angel's faces went from surprise and confusion to pain and then finally into the serenity of love when he delivered them into heaven.

* * *

Adrian finished his shift at Big Value, the mornings thoughts swimming around and around in his mind. He went to the Dixons electrical store and bought himself a handheld camera and video recorder. It was small enough to fit in his pocket so he could carry it around with him wherever he went. He made his way to the library, not bothering to stop off at home; he didn't want his mother to sour his day. As he sat in his favourite chair in the library, he manoeuvred his camera to the side of his leg. By positioning it just right he believed he would be able to take footage of what delights lay hidden under Tiffany's skirt. He sat back with a book he had just grabbed from a shelf on his way in; looking at it now he wished he had bothered to choose a book, he was not going to enjoy the next few hours in the company of Bubbles Blower, 'My Story.' Adrian tried to read it but even he didn't have the patience to read the autobiography of an air-headed porn star, so had to pick up his camera and go hunt for a proper book. He took his time then settled for a novel about a dog, the content wasn't really that important but he would rather flick through that than see images of Bubble's triumphs in the porn industry.

Adrian settled into his book, his camera once again primed and ready for the arrival of Tiffany. She turned up at about 4pm and smiled at Adrian as she sat down.

"Hi." Adrian said, "How are you today?"

"Ok," said Tiffany.

Both settled into their chairs; Tiffany took out her books and pens and Adrian surreptitiously pressed record on his camera. Inside he had butterflies in his stomach and was filled with anticipation. The hunt was on, he thought, it may take a bit of time but time he had plenty of. He had Tiffany on his hook now and he was prepared to take things at her pace, because when his time came; the pace, the place and the girl would be solely on *his* terms.

Jocasta

Chapter 18

'Pure love and suspicion cannot dwell together; at the door where the latter enters, the former makes its exit.'

Alexandre Dumas Pere

April 2012

Jocasta was lonely. Every morning she would wake up, still in the same bedroom with the same bed, same curtains, same carpet and same lumpy, hairy, ugly body she lived in.

Adrian was a man now, no longer in need of his mother's love and attention. When at home he would adhere to her joint meals, although that was the only concession he made towards her and the meals were often eaten in silence; Adrian eating so fast Jocasta believed he barely tasted the food she so lovingly prepared for him.

Where Jocasta had spent the last twenty years contenting herself with being a mother, her constant solitude and feelings of uselessness were now becoming hard to bear. If Jocasta had ever been accepted by people, she believed she could have been the life and soul of any party. She remembered fondly her month in Mykonos, her time with Avram and her nights of fun and passion with him.

Jocasta knew it was time for her to cut the cords with Adrian, to accept he had become a man, to be proud of what she had achieved as a mother and to allow herself to move on and at last have a life to remember. As she was still on benefits, Jocasta knew it wasn't so simple as to pack her bags and make for somewhere hot. She needed to get back into employment and needed to get trained on computers. There was no way she could apply for a job if she didn't know how to put words in Windows or put a boot up wherever it was they put it. Jocasta got dressed and resolved to visit the job centre where she could be put onto training courses to get what she needed, to go back out into the world of the living.

* * *

16th May 2012
12:00 hours

Having spent the last month on a Windows 8, PowerPoint and Excel training programme at the Adult Learning Centre, Jocasta was beginning to feel like a human being again; no longer just a mother but an adult who was capable of work, holding down their own and contributing towards society. It gave

Mother Be The Judge

her a great self-respect and she was proud of what she had achieved. Jocasta had passed the course with flying colours; the computer which had filled her with apprehension when she first sat in front of it was actually the friendliest thing she'd met in her whole life. There were no special codes or convoluted equations as she had imagined; the computer spoke English, everything was clear with 'help' just a click of a button away. She had flown through the tasks set for her by the tutor and had begun a very loving relationship with the hard drive of the Hewlett Packard allocated to her. Jocasta could not believe she had spent so much of her life in solitude when a computer had been in Adrian's room for the last eight years. She lamented the stuff she had missed because she hadn't taken the World Wide Highway many moons ago.

Jocasta was beginning to understand what it meant to be an adult again; it wasn't just about being a mother. Life didn't have to stop just because someone else was dependent on you. People can and *did* enjoy the best of both worlds. Feeling ready to step out into mankind and hopeful she may actually make some friends, Jocasta began to hunt for a job. As she had previously worked in a doctor's surgery, that's where Jocasta started looking. Several C.V.s and hundreds of job applications later and Jocasta now found herself waiting for an interview just around the corner from where she lived.

* * *

Jocasta had taken her time getting ready for the interview; having had nothing to get dressed up for in the past twenty years, her wardrobe was limited to black leggings and baggy tops, all bought in Big Value and none which could pass for smart. Jocasta didn't think a t-shirt proclaiming, 'Elvis is King', was very appropriate either so decided she had to visit the local store and spend some of her emergency money. She visited Primani which was within her budget and found a plus size range which she could squeeze her now hefty bulk into. Loneliness had many downsides and eating for comfort was probably the worst. No food item lasted long in Jocasta's kitchen and her body was paying the price. Thankfully Primani sympathised with the larger woman and Jocasta was able to buy a pair of black trousers and three smart tops for less than twenty pounds. Jocasta gave a silent thank you for Chinese sweatshops as she had paid for her items at the till.

* * *

The Human Resources Manager approached Jocasta with a smile, holding out her hand in anticipation of a handshake.

"Jocasta Brown?" She asked.

"Yes, Hi," said Jocasta, shaking the outstretched hand. She felt sick with nerves; this was an experience she hadn't had since she had first applied for a similar

Mother Be The Judge

position more than thirty years ago. She was determined to start a new phase in her life, however, so she smiled back, took a deep breath and followed the manager into an office for the interview which would determine her future as not just Adrian's mother, but an independent woman.

The interview went on for about half an hour and Jocasta felt she had answered all the questions well. She remembered a lot of what went on in her previous job; well, it had consumed her life at the time. It seemed the only thing that had changed since *her* time was that the appointments were made on the computer. Everything else remained the same, they still held paper records for the patients and were still expected to keep the patients away from the doctors unless absolutely necessary. Unbelievably Jocasta was offered the job on the spot. The manager had told her that it was nice to interview someone so keen and who had an obvious passion for the work. She was asked to return the following Monday for staff training and to pick up her new I.D card.

* * *

Jocasta waddled home as fast as her chubby legs could carry her, she couldn't wait to cook a lovely dinner and surprise Adrian with her news. Jocasta knew how much she had relied on Adrian in the past years and could understand he found her somewhat of a burden. She was happy to now be able to offer Adrian his freedom from her and hoped it may bring them closer. She thought if they both lived their lives as equals now - both working adults - then they could exchange stories about their working day. Conversations would be enjoyable and she could contribute more to them, rather than giving a blow by blow account of how she had cleaned and scrubbed the flat or how she had put a new duvet cover on in under two minutes. Jocasta arrived at the flat and called out Adrian's name; it was nearly 4pm and he would usually be home although he had been spending longer and longer at the library these days.

Wanting to show Adrian her now proficient skills on the computer and feeling uber confident in herself, Jocasta decided to take an unusual step and go into Adrian's bedroom. She would surprise him by giving it a thorough clean as she was certain he would not have ever pulled out the bed and cleared the build of up of dust and cobwebs which would be under there, along with errant socks and mouldy half eaten sandwiches. Then she intended to go onto Adrian's computer and produce a banner heralding her new work appointment.

She dragged the hoover into the room and retrieved her polish and duster from under the sink, then set about cleaning. Jocasta knew Adrian may be a bit put out that she had broken his rule of no entry, but intended to do such a good job he would forgive her indiscretion.

Jocasta started with picking up the dirty clothes

from the floor, then moved onto cleaning small bits of rubbish; receipts, crisp packets etc. taking them out of the room in a black bag. She polished the window sill and the tops of Adrian's chest of drawers then set about changing his grey bed sheets, made all the greyer because she knew he hadn't changed them for over a month despite her relentless pleading for him to put the sheets in the wash. Jocasta pulled out the single bed and found a Scooby Doo figure jammed into the space between the headboard and the mattress; she remembered fondly Adrian's face when he had opened that particular present. Jocasta moved the bed further but it stuck in the confines of the room. She realised the only way to get the bed completely out of the way was to remove the mattress and split the bottom of the Divan where its base was held together by a brass fitting. She heaved the heavy mattress off the bed and pushed it out into the hallway then turned back to look at the bed's base, ready to tackle the fitting.

What Jocasta saw lying on the rectangle of wood and cloth, made her stop in her tracks. A pair of pink knickers lay on top of a magazine. Jocasta heard a rush of blood in her ears and her subconscious screamed at her to turn and walk away, but she couldn't. She reached for the knickers, putting her two hands in the waistband and pulling them open so she could gauge the size of them. It was clear and the label confirmed to her that they belonged to a child of ten to eleven years. Looking down once again, Jocasta now reached for the shiny pages of the magazine which proclaimed, 'Barely Legal' on the front cover. Opening the front page,

Jocasta's eyes were assaulted by pictures of what could only be described as girls, or at least women pretending to be girls, dressed in school uniforms and flashing their hairless vaginas for all of the world to see.

Flashbacks from Savannah West hit Jocasta's brain like a turbulent storm sending not only images of Adrian's wet legged entrance into their flat but the images now gave aggressive and explicit suggestions as to how Adrian may be responsible for Savannah's death.

Jocasta stood and replaced the knickers and magazine, then covered it with the mattress. Working on autopilot now, she put on the new sheets, hoovered the room then left, closing Adrian's door behind her. She went into the kitchen and cooked Adrian's dinner, no longer thinking to make anything special. She put the dinner on the table and then sat in her spot awaiting the arrival of her son. It was time to face the truth.

* * *

4pm came and went with no sign of Adrian. Jocasta ate her dinner and then ate Adrian's dinner also as she could think of nothing else to do. She cleared the plates and put the dirty dishes into the sink then slowly washed them. As her hands made their circular movements around the plates, Jocasta considered what she had found. The magazine was one which was readily available on the top shelf of any newsagents; she had seen them stacked there every time she had perused the shelves. Had this been her only find, Jocasta could imagine herself tittering at Adrian's cheekiness and congratulating herself that at least he wasn't gay. The knickers on the other hand, she had trouble excusing. They were definitely meant for a ten year old girl, the label had confirmed that. The knickers could belong to anyone. They may have been found in the street or even stolen by Adrian from Big Value. Jocasta couldn't shake the image of Adrian's wet legs from her mind; this seemed to be the one factor which tied the whole thing together. It was so hard for Jocasta to allow these seeds of suspicion into her mind. There were big barriers surrounding that part of her brain; keeping good thoughts in and bad thoughts out, but these circumstances had been like a sledgehammer smashing the barriers down.

Now Jocasta considered Savannah, the little girl she had never brought to mind before; preferring instead to concentrate on Adrian's plight. Savannah, the sweet little girl she had seen in the playground; that had been with Lacey when Adrian had sent them a paper plane; yet another memory which Jocasta had buried in her unwillingness to blame Adrian. That poor Savannah, who had been brutally raped and murdered, possibly at the hands of her own son. Fragile Savannah who's life had been taken away from her, never again would she play or sing or talk or laugh a sweet laugh. Jocasta then focused her attention on Savannah's mother. She remembered how it felt when Adrian had been sick in hospital. How desperately upset and useless she felt and how physically the pain of loss had affected her. Jocasta knew Savannah's mother must wake daily lamenting the loss of her daughter, seeing her face in everything which reminded her of Savannah; every TV programme she had loved, every drink she enjoyed, every time she had sat in the now empty chair around the dining table. Savannah's mother had lost her very reason for existing; Jocasta would not have blamed her if she had committed suicide as she couldn't imagine her own life without Adrian in it. She wondered how all of this could possibly have happened. Where did Adrian get his desires from? Jocasta had never even discussed the facts of life with him, preferring to let the school undertake that particular task. How had a sweet, loving, good child become a depraved, vile and evil beast? Nothing had happened in Adrian's life for him to feel the need to rebel; he had every whim catered to, he was never abused, never smacked and *never* told, 'No'.

Jocasta could only bring it down to one factor - her. It must be *her* fault. It was her DNA, her blood running through Adrian's body. She had carried him, given birth to him and nurtured him, the only reason he was physically able to carry out these vile acts was because of the limbs she had created for him. No, she decided, it wasn't Adrian's fault; it was hers. She was the devil, it was the only explanation. Jocasta decided the only thing which saved this whole situation was that nothing had happened since Savannah's death. No further child had gone missing. No one had come

Mother Be The Judge

knocking on her door accusing Adrian of wrongdoing. It was very possible that Savannah's death had been a mistake, a terrible tragedy never meant to happen. Adrian must have been devastated to know he had committed a cardinal sin, the worst sin any human could commit. Jocasta realised her poor Adrian had had to carry the burden of his guilt for the last four years, never able to share what happened for fear no one could understand. Believing this, was the only way Jocasta could make herself breathe again. The only way her heart could beat and she could retain any love for her son. She had to believe this was all one catastrophic mistake and whilst no other girls were hurt and no mistakes were made, Jocasta resolved to keep Adrian's secret. She didn't want to broach the subject with him, one, because she didn't feel able to soothe the pain he must feel knowing he was party to such a terrible accident and, two, because she was frightened Adrian might tell her a truth she didn't really want to hear. It was going to take her a long time to forgive Adrian this sin, she could feel tendrils of love recoiling away from Adrian and springing back into her heart. It would serve her better to forget this suspicion or her love may gradually turn to hate.

Reaching for the chocolate, Jocasta chose to lose herself in some gorging of the brown loveliness. As she felt the warm glow of chocolate fill the hole in her soul, Jocasta gave a silent prayer that she was doing the right thing.

Adrian

Chapter 19

'Evil is unspectacular and always human and shares our bed and eats at our own table.'
W.H. Auden, Herman Melville.

16th May 2012
15:30 hours

Adrian sat in his favourite chair inside the library, waiting for Tiffany to show. He didn't know for definite that she would be there, he had made a concerted effort to keep all contact with her confined to the library. All the shows he had watched on television told him that computers could be checked, CCTV could be found in all corners of the atmos. and people loved to give their two pennies to the Press and *then* to the police.

His spot in the library was chosen not only because it was near to the study tables but also because it was out of sight of the surveillance camera. As a library was rarely a conduit for violence, the camera had been placed in the main reception just because it was *de rigueur;* it served no real purpose and only covered the entrance and exit of library visitors. Adrian didn't know where the CCTV's blind spots were but knew there was no way it covered the area he frequented.

Adrian wondered if today would be the day that Tiffany gave herself to him. She had visited him in the library every week day since that first conversation. They spoke and laughed with each other, Adrian would listen to Tiffany's daily woes and her agony at the hands of the bullies. He would console and cushion the emotional blows, buoying Tiffany's confidence with compliments; she had even commented that nobody understood her the way he did and he had encouraged this way of thinking. When he had reached over to place his hand on Tiffany's knee she had not recoiled, in fact she had not even registered his touch with anything other than a slight smile. Adrian had then waited a day before professing his affection for Tiffany. He told her that no one came close to her and that she was the most beautiful girl he had ever seen. He thought he may have pushed his luck making that extravagant comment; surely Tiffany owned a mirror. Tiffany *had* rolled her eyes, but accepted the compliment in the spirit it was offered. After a few weeks Adrian realised that he really did love Tiffany. She was so caring and funny, able to smile every day despite the merciless torture at the hands of her bullies. He admired her for her ability to switch from a bullied wretch to a smiling confidante in his presence. Adrian had finally, joyfully, found the girl who would fulfil his fantasy; she would unlock the hidden treasure and allow him to experience the explosive release of passion and desire. She was 'the one', of that he was certain.

* * *

16:00 hours

Tiffany arrived at the library. She was animated as she reached her usual study table, immediately engaging Adrian in conversation; her shyness in the earlier days had vanished now that she had an affinity with him.

"Hi Adrian," she enthused, "How was Big Value today?"

"Yeah it was alright." Adrian looked downhearted as he shifted his gaze from tome to Tiffany.

"Oh, what's wrong?" Tiffany asked, she immediately sensed that Adrian was not in his usual affable mood.

"I got sacked from Big Value," lied Adrian, crinkling his chin so the dimples of crying would appear.

"Oh, how did that happen?" Tiffany made to leave her chair but stopped when Adrian lifted his hand as if to ward off her advances.

"I just made a silly mistake." He informed her, "All I did was put the broccoli where the cauliflower should be, the manager doesn't like me. She was looking for any excuse to get rid of me."

Tiffany could relate to that; any bad mark she

received from tutors she always put down to the fact that they didn't like her.

"What are you going to do?" She asked him.

"I don't know, my mum is going to kill me." Adrian now began to cry in earnest, all pretence of stoicism lost in his dismay. He silently patted himself on the back for doing such a good acting job.

"Oh Adrian, I just want to cuddle you." Tiffany said, she yearned to leave her chair and put her arms around him.

"You can't do that in here Tiffany." Adrian told her. "I've told you before, people would think it was weird someone your age cuddling someone my age. You know how horrible people can be, they would never understand."

"I don't care what people think." Tiffany said. "It's only a cuddle, you could be my brother; how would they know?"

"The librarian knows my mother." Adrian lied again. "If she saw us cuddling she would think there was something wrong and then you would never be allowed to come to the library again."

Tiffany couldn't bear the thought of being denied seeing the one person in the world who made her feel good. She desperately wanted to comfort the boy who had been more understanding than her father and more loving than even her mother. She felt so grown up now she was eleven. She was capable of so many things, proficient in most things adult - cooking, cleaning, reading and writing. In Africa and other such countries children of her age lead adult lives and brought up younger siblings, she had seen it on the telly. Tiffany was cross that her age was preventing her from taking full advantage of her new found love. She decided if she could not console Adrian in a public place then she would find somewhere else. Somewhere away from the prying eyes of adults who thought they understood what was going on and who thought that Adrian wanted more from her than just her friendship. Tiffany believed she knew better. Adrian was her one true friend, the person who had lifted her from the depths of despair and who day by day restored in her the flames her bullies had extinguished.

"Why don't we go outside?" she asked him.

"What for?" asked Adrian back. He wanted to be certain it was Tiffany's idea to leave the library; he didn't want her to feel trapped in any way.

"Yeah come on." Tiffany replied, "We don't have to stay here, why don't we go to the park and then we can talk without nosy people looking at us." Tiffany stood and began to put back the books she had taken out of her bag.

"Where will we go?" asked Adrian.

"We can go to the park; there are loads of benches there."

And people, thought Adrian; "I know a better place." He said, "What time do you have to be home?"

"5:30 for dinner."

"Ok, well we can get there on the bus and then get a bus back."

Adrian got out of his chair then remembered buses had CCTV. He had intended to take Tiffany to a wooded area in Olinsbury Heath but had almost made a terrible error of judgement by travelling together with Tiffany on a bus.

"Have you got a mobile phone?" He asked Tiffany, fingers crossed and breath held awaiting her response.

"Yeah, my mum gave it to me for emergencies, why?"

"Oh, just in case we're late and you have to ring your parents." He began to walk to the library doors, staying ahead of Tiffany so they didn't look like they were together. He had changed his mind about where to go with Tiffany. The one sure way to evade capture was to go somewhere deserted away from the prying technological eye of cameras. Somewhere Adrian could be free to do what he wanted and where he could have Tiffany without always looking over his shoulder wondering whether she had been discovered yet. Although he had used it before, the allotment was the perfect place for what he wanted; it was even more deserted now than it had been four years ago. Some people had given up their allotments, not being able to dig and sow knowing a girl may have been killed on that very piece of soil where their cabbages grew. There was no CCTV, the unused plots were full of heavy vegetation and Adrian rarely saw visitors to the allotments on a week day; gardening it seemed was a weekend pursuit. Adrian had also invented a way to stop people searching for Tiffany; having a mobile phone belonging to her and given her parents refusal to accept Tiffany was bullied, Adrian had now planned to keep in contact with Tiffany's parents for as long as he could, purporting to *be* Tiffany. He would let them think she had run away but was safe and well and not wanting to be found. This should delay any search parties and snoopers and stop the police coming to his door.

He got outside the library and turned to see Tiffany just coming out of the doors. She looked up at him and gave a sunshine smile. It pleased Adrian that Tiffany was glad to be in his company. An overwhelming feeling of love came over him and he reached out to Tiffany, only managing to pull himself together and get his hand away from her at the last minute.

"Not here." He said as her hand was left empty. "Come on, I know a place."

They walked together, Adrian chatting about carrots and cabbage, Tiffany talking about school and bullies. A few times Adrian realised he was speaking about work in the present tense and was worried Tiffany may discover his lie but her age meant suspicion was not yet a learnt habit so she walked on oblivious to his mistakes.

"Adrian please slow down." Tiffany called out to him. In his excitement at what was to come and his desire to not be seen with Tiffany, Adrian had walked a lot faster than Tiffany and was almost about to turn the corner whereas she was still fifty metres behind him. Adrian wanted to keep Tiffany interested so slowed at the corner of Twockford Road and waited for her to catch up before they turned into Migdon Lane. Although there was a shopping complex on the opposite side of the road, Adrian was happy there was

Mother Be The Judge

no CCTV on the residential side of the street where they walked together. Adrian and Tiffany continued to walk side by side along Migdon Lane, both with their noses curled up in distaste at the smells emanating from the nearby sewage plant. Because Adrian lived in the area, he rarely smelt the vile smell, his nose being used to it, but today was hot and windy, the perfect combination for the sewers to really impress the nose.

"Oh that's bad," said Tiffany.

"It wasn't me," said Adrian, lifting his eyebrows in mock innocence. Tiffany giggled and they both continued to walk into the shadow of the rugby ground and down the alleyway leading to the allotments.

"What is this place?" enquired Tiffany.

"It's gardens." Adrian told her. "People who don't have one can pay for a square and then plant stuff on them."

"Oh, I didn't know you could do that," said Tiffany.

"Yeah, I'm getting one." Adrian said. "But my mate owns this one." He led her to his favourite blue shed with the cast iron bench outside. "He lets me sit here and sometimes I dig for him."

"Cool." Said Tiffany and looked as if she actually meant it. It pleased Adrian; he felt he had made the right choice. Tiffany was a wonderful caring person who didn't mock him and liked the things that he liked.

"I love you Tiffany." Adrian blurted out. The air seemed to still in the space between them.

"I love you too." Tiffany said and smiled up into Adrian's face.

Adrian was shocked. It had been a mistake to proclaim his love for her, she could have walked away, but her acceptance of his love and confirmation of her own made Adrian's heart sing with joy.

"We shouldn't be in love though." He told her, "I am older than you, no one will understand."

He sat on the bench and patted the space beside him, inviting Tiffany to sit alongside. She did so immediately.

"I don't care about other people." Tiffany said, "I don't care about my age either." And she didn't, Tiffany didn't feel eleven. She didn't know what it was to *feel* eighteen, but found it hard to believe it would feel much different. Tiffany knew her feelings for Adrian were real; he had been her shoulder to cry on, the only one who understood her, who didn't treat her like a child. She had definite feelings for Adrian and had no problem identifying those feelings as love.

"When you are older we can run away together." Adrian told her. He turned his body towards her and rested his arm along the back of the bench. Tiffany moved into the space created by Adrian's arm moving; pushing herself up into his body and allowing Adrian's arm to cuddle around her. She enjoyed the warm feeling, both physical and emotional, which she got from his embrace.

"Why don't we run away now?" asked Tiffany and she meant it. She really did feel as though her place was meant to be with Adrian. She knew she was too young to get married and have children but she thought Adrian may wait for her. As long as they were together that's all that mattered.

Adrian took a deep long breath through his nose. Tiffany was now close enough he could smell her. He took in the flowery aroma of her shampoo and continued to smell her feminine odour, even imagining he could smell a slight whiff of urine from her, probably where she hadn't wiped herself properly. Adrian found himself becoming aroused, his penis was hardening in anticipation and he had to work hard not to touch himself in front of Tiffany. She wasn't ready for that yet.

"We will run away together then." Said Adrian, "But first you have to prove you love me."

"How can I do that?" asked Tiffany.

"Well you can kiss me." Adrian told her.

Tiffany had never kissed anyone before, but she wanted to kiss Adrian. She thought this would show him that she really loved him and then they could be together, just the two of them. She lifted her head in Adrian's direction and puckered her lips to await his tender kiss.

Adrian looked at Tiffany's pink lips puckered up before him. He felt the desire heat in the soles of his feet and begin to rise through the very marrow of his bones, filling each pore of his being. It built and swelled, pushing its way past his already swollen penis, his heart hammered in his chest, his lungs drew in deep breaths. The desire in him continued to work its way up to his throat causing him to let loose a low growl. His eyes rolled in their sockets and once again he felt as though he was watching a scene playing out in front of him. The snuff movie he had been writing in his mind for the last four years since Savannah's death now began to play out before him.

* * *

He kissed Tiffany roughly on the lips. She pulled away, not liking the stubbly feel on her soft lips. "Adrian." She began to protest but then saw in front of her not the boy she had fallen in love with but a daemon. Adrian's eyes were rolling in his head and his face had taken on an evil expression. "Adrian what's wrong?" Tiffany asked, she thought maybe he had hurt himself. Suddenly Adrian reached out and grabbed Tiffany around the throat, his fingers dug tightly into her neck and Tiffany realised she had made a huge mistake. Adrian didn't love her, he was the stranger her parents had always warned her about; the big bad wolf that blew the house down and ate Little Red Riding Hood's grandma. Adrian was squeezing harder and harder and Tiffany was also vaguely aware of an intrusion in her private area. The light in Tiffany's eyes began to form a tunnel with just Adrian's face at the end of it. She tried to get some words out of her mouth, she wanted to plead with Adrian to stop what he was doing, but no words could get out. Tiffany's last thoughts strangely were of her pet mouse she had

had when she was five. It was the first death she had ever experienced and she had wondered at the time if her mouse had gone to the same heaven people went to. Tiffany knew she was about to find out for herself. She concentrated on looking at Adrian's face hoping he would see her plea and stop this dreadful act. He looked intently at her, waiting for the moment when her lights went out.

* * *

'Mum, I'm not coming home 2day. I can't take the bullying any more so have run away. I luv u x x'

Adrian put Tiffany's phone into his jeans pocket then continued to wrap her up in the green tarpaulin he had stolen off an allotment. He picked her up in his arms and moved her over to an abandoned patch, then using a shovel he had taken from the blue shed; he dug a deep ditch to lay Tiffany to rest. On each dig Adrian relived flashes of what he had just done. Dig; him pushing his penis into Tiffany's slack, dead mouth. Dig; him biting into Tiffany's flesh, tasting the sweetness of her blood. Dig; the sweet release as Adrian reached the climax he had sought for so long. Adrian spent the next half hour digging deeper and deeper, wallowing in his deed. No part of him felt remorse or regret; he believed in his love for Tiffany and was convinced he had fulfilled both his and Tiffany's destiny. Once the hole was deep enough, he lay Tiffany in her final resting place and waved her a fond goodbye before replenishing the earth he had removed. It was getting dark and Adrian was feeling hungry. He walked away from Tiffany's grave and gave a silent curse as he realised he hadn't filmed himself with her. Once again he had gottten carried away in the moment. Adrian decided he would have to plan things better the next time an angel came to him.

He sauntered along the road wondering what shitty meal his mother had concocted; all thoughts of Tiffany now wiped from his mind and replaced with visions of a warm dinner.

Chapter 20

'A mother loves her children even when they least deserve to be loved.'
Kate Semperi 'Mothers'

16th May 2012
18:30 hours

Jocasta sat at the table still waiting for Adrian to arrive home. She had finished all the chocolate in the cupboard and had also eaten three packets of salt and vinegar crisps, some crackers with pate and was now considering something sweet to combat the savoury taste in her mouth. She tried to keep only thoughts of food in her head so she wouldn't have to dwell in the whirlpool of suspicion her find in Adrian's bedroom had instilled in her.

Jocasta was battling with her conscience; she couldn't shake the image of Savannah's mother from her mind. Imagining what she must be feeling at the loss of her child was causing Jocasta real heartache. She remembered again how she felt when Adrian was sick, how images of his dead body would flash in her mind. To lose Adrian would be a devastating blow, her world would be turned upside down and all her reasons for breathing would disappear in the blink of an eye. Savannah's mother was often seen by Jocasta, staggering around the Fern Bridge estate; her son Andrew following in her wake. Mae West was the shell of the woman she had once been, her skin had taken on a yellow tinge where her liver wasn't able to cope with the incessant battering from alcohol. Andrew was a lost little boy, no longer cared for by his bigger sister and not able to take over the role of carer for the drunken mother. Mike the step father was nowhere to be seen; suspicion had pushed its way into his relationship with Mae and she was unable to coexist with a person she believed possibly involved in the murder of her daughter.

Now believing that Adrian was in some way the cause of the pain Savannah's family lived with, Jocasta felt the weight of responsibility heavy on her shoulders. She had an overwhelming urge to go and visit Savannah's family, to help them with their pain and to make recompense for the loss that had been forced upon them. Only her love for Adrian kept her firmly anchored in her kitchen chair; no amount of grief or guilt could take away her adoration of him. She knew Adrian was a good person and believed it must have been a terrible accident. Jocasta had finally come to the decision that she was going to confront Adrian about Savannah. She would not allow herself to shy away from her responsibility as Adrian's mother. He was suffering a terrible burden of guilt and it was her role to relive that burden. Adrian should be allowed to speak and offload his burden onto her. She would take his woes onto her shoulders and comfort him.

Jocasta heard the front door open and turned to welcome Adrian who was walking towards her.

"What's for dinner?" Adrian asked.

"I ate it," said Jocasta. "You weren't here and it got cold."

Adrian turned into the bathroom and called out from behind the door. "Can you make me something then, I'm just having a shower."

"In the middle of the day?"

"Yeah, I've had a busy day." Adrian smiled to himself as he began to remove his clothing, keeping Tiffany's blue knickers tightly in his hand as he walked into the shower.

Jocasta got up from the table and rushed to retrieve the knickers she had found earlier under Adrian's bed. She made a quick egg and chips and put them on the table, then sat with the knickers secreted in her hand waiting for Adrian to finish his shower.

* * *

Adrian washed himself using his newly acquired knickers as a flannel. He spent a long time reliving the moment that life had left Tiffany and serenity had set in. Adrian felt like a God and realised his real pleasure was in the taking of life. The carnal pleasure he got after the act of killing was like his reward for bestowing the gift of peace on Tiffany. No longer would his angel suffer at the hands of bullies or bad parenting, he had delivered her from evil. Adrian finished his shower, wrapped himself in a towel, returned to his room and quickly started to put on his pyjamas. He threw Tiffany's knickers into his desk drawer; they would have to dry before he could put them in his hiding place under the mattress. As Adrian dressed he noticed that his sheets had been changed and the usual detritus was missing from his now clean room. The Pig had been inside his inner sanctum. He lifted the mattress to check what was underneath and found Savannah's knickers were missing. Adrian realised that the Pig must have found them; he wondered what she must be thinking. He walked from his room and saw his mother sitting back at the kitchen table, a plate of food awaited him and he could see her hands held tightly together in her lap. Uncertain how to approach the situation because he didn't know what his mother may suspect, Adrian decided to play the long game and allow the Pig to play her hand first.

"Egg and chips," he stated as he sat at the table, and then began to eat in his usual silence. Butterflies fluttered in his stomach in anticipation at what was to come; would his mother have the guts to confront him, he wondered.

"Adrian I need to ask you something." Jocasta said.

"What?" he stopped eating; placed his knife and fork on the plate and sat back in his chair. Jocasta put her clenched hands onto the table and then slowly opened them allowing the pink material to drop onto the table. As there was no element of surprise for Adrian, he remained level in both expression and manner. He decided to say nothing; he wanted to hear what his mother would say.

"Adrian I found these today when I was cleaning your room for you. I know I shouldn't have gone in there but I got a new job today and was feeling happy so wanted to do something for you." Jocasta looked at the table, unable to stare into Adrian's eyes; she didn't want to see the reproach that must be in them. She took a deep breath and continued.

"When I moved the bed these knickers were there with that disgusting magazine. Please tell me why you have them, where did you get them from?"

Adrian knew Jocasta was asking him to give her a reasonable explanation for why he possessed such an item. She wanted him to soothe her fears, tell her some inane story for why he had them so she could retreat back into her world of ignorance and continue to love him unquestioningly. But today Adrian was a God; today Adrian had achieved the climax of love which his mother had tried to take away from him when she had allowed doctors to remove his most masculine part. Today Adrian was going to let his mother know just what he had done to little Savannah - not Tiffany, he was not ready to share her yet. He was going to give his mother a blow by blow account of every minute detail of Savannah's demise. He was going to let her know it was her fault and that she had turned him into the person he was today. Adrian *had* been carrying this tale around with him but it wasn't a burden. It was like a Gospel which needed to be written, a story to be heralded; his magnificent achievement in creating angels. Love in its purest form - death making it eternal.

Adrian told his mother everything that had happened between himself and Savannah. He stopped her when she tried to excuse the death as an accident and reminded her that Savannah was not only murdered but raped, sodomised and bitten. He reminded her of how he had joined the search party and found Savannah's body; how he had delivered Savannah into the hands of the police and told his mother why that was such a clever thing to do.

"And you." he accused, "You knew. You spoke to that copper and told him I was with you that night. You *knew* I had killed Savannah, just like you knew I had touched Charmaine. I *told* you I had touched her and you wouldn't listen. You did this, it's your fault you fucking stupid cunt." Adrian spat out the last word. He had become progressively louder and more animated as he relived his story and anger had swelled in him as he realised that he did actually blame his mother for some of what had happened. Maybe if she had reprimanded him in the police station all those years ago he would have some sense of right and wrong. If she hadn't have bought him a computer he definitely wouldn't have learnt so much or been able to communicate with Savannah like he had.

Jocasta took every word of Adrian's rant like a target receives an arrow. Each word hit home deep and hard. The barriers of denial were torn from their foundations in her brain and were replaced with dark truths; sharp, clear images of the evil deeds Adrian had committed buried themselves deep into Jocasta's brain. Now embedded, they were never going to leave. Every possible excuse Jocasta had consoled herself with in the past was ripped away from her. Jocasta felt empty, she had nothing inside her but a void of desperation. She didn't know what to say to Adrian; how could she make things go back to the way they had been before she had opened her mouth and confronted a truth which she hadn't wanted to hear? She knew there was no way back, her son was a monster, a beast that preyed on young girls. A dark daemon whose desire in life was to rape, maim and murder sweet innocent children.

"Adrian, you must tell the police what you have done," whispered Jocasta.

Adrian looked at Jocasta in disbelief, "Are you actually listening to me Pig?" he slammed the table with the palm of his hand, causing Jocasta to jump in her chair. "I just told you, all of this is *your* fault. You have been a bad mother, a dirty whore who gave herself to the first man who paid her any attention. You are a loser, you have no friends, you are ugly, you made me ugly and you let the doctors *destroy* me. If I was normal this wouldn't have happened." Adrian walked around the table and put his hands around his mother's chubby, clammy neck. He yearned to squeeze the life out of her right there at the kitchen table but knew there was no way he could get away with it and prided himself on having more self-control than that. Instead he held her in a firm embrace and then leant down to whisper in her ear.

"And now you want to send me away to prison where I will be beaten and fucked by big hairy monsters. You want to send me away from you so you can have the life you always wanted without me in it. You did this to me and now you're making me go. I thought you loved me."

Jocasta began to weep. She wept for Savannah, she wept for Savannah's parents and she also wept for Adrian. Could it be true that it was really all her fault? Everything Adrian had just accused her of was true; maybe if she had fought harder to save Adrian from having his testicles removed then he would be leading a normal healthy sex life. She knew that at the time when he was sick, the doctors had told her it was the best thing to do, but had she really bothered to question them? No, she had blindly accepted what they had told her; the same way she had blindly accepted Adrian's innocence in all things because she loved him. And she did love him; she loved him so much it hurt. Jocasta knew that Adrian had committed a grievous sin, but she agreed with him that if he went to prison then he would probably suffer daily at the hands people with evil in their veins. No matter what Adrian had done, she couldn't bear to think of him being tortured and also could not bear to consider him out of her own life. If Adrian went to prison he would be dead to her, she would be alone again with only her guilt and disgust to keep her company.

"What are we going to do Adrian?" She asked; "That poor child."

"She was no child." Adrian sneered. "You know what those girls are like on the estate."

"Well they do dress like little tarts." Jocasta agreed.

Adrian could see that Jocasta was now looking for him to guide her in what she should do next. Her momentary mention of police was had been quickly scuppered with his imagery of being tortured by the inmates. Adrian could see that his mother *wanted* him to manipulate the situation. She wanted him to put the words into her mouth which would make everything go back to normal. He knew now why he despised her; she was probably enjoying all the attention he was giving her right now. It didn't matter that they were discussing a subject most other people found abhorrent, any attention from Adrian was good attention in his mother's eyes.

"Listen mummy, I'm sorry for everything that has happened. To be honest I don't know why I did it. I think I'm sick. I need help. People outside won't understand, I need you to help me mummy." Adrian knelt on the floor of the kitchen and put his head on his mother's knee. Jocasta's hands recoiled from where they had been placed and she sat, silently waving them in the air, not knowing where to place them. Eventually her maternal instinct took over and she put her hands on Adrian's head, running her fingers through his hair like she had done when he was a child.

"Ok Adrian, I will help you." She said silently. Adrian gave a hidden grin, believing he had won and had been able to manipulate his mother once again. He silently rocked backwards and forwards at his mother's knee, enjoying her embrace and considering how he would continue in his endeavours with his angels. He thought it may even be possible to start to bring the girls to his house now that his mother was so firmly on his side, but that would take a lot of planning and a lot of manipulation. He started to hum an old nursery rhyme his mother used to sing him every night; he thought it would be useful to remind her of the love she had for him at every possible opportunity.

* * *

Jocasta listened to Adrian humming and felt the bristles of his hair. She looked blankly at the wall, however, deep in thought at how she was going to help Adrian. When she had made that promise to him, she actually meant that she would help him to never commit his foul crimes again. Her love for Adrian as her son had not dissipated, she still adored the very bones of him, but Jocasta was a good person. She knew that what Adrian had done to Savannah was the most heinous of crimes. There was nothing in Jocasta that could excuse or forgive what Adrian had done. Now that he had admitted his sins to Jocasta, she had nothing to take the images of Savannah away from her. She once again considered Savannah's mother and the terrible pain which Jocasta's own flesh and blood had bestowed upon her. Jocasta knew it was her duty now as Adrian's mother to ensure that he

Mother Be The Judge

would never again commit any atrocities. Whilst she knew she could not commit him to a life in prison, Jocasta decided she could keep Adrian in her own home grown version of one. She started her new job on Monday; it would be the perfect place to research medicines which she could give to Adrian to control his urges and to keep him at home. Jocasta did not believe Adrian was safe to be out on the streets any longer. He needed to be protected from the desires he could not control. Children had to be protected from him and Jocasta knew it was now her role to ensure that she kept the children safe. No more would the fruit of her blackened womb be allowed to hurt. No more would he be allowed to kill. She would do her job and she would do it well. Jocasta promised herself that she would make things right and keep her baby at home where he belonged.

"Adrian," she said. He turned around on the floor and sat down with his legs crossed, looking up into her eyes. Jocasta looked at his face and saw in it the sweet boy who had grown up her only friend.

"Adrian, what you did was wrong; you should never have hurt that poor baby. But you are right, maybe you are sick. I am not going to call the police because I believe you are sorry." Adrian leant forward and cuddled Jocasta's leg, once again placing his head on her lap. She took his face in both hands and moved it back then leant down so they were face to face.

"But Adrian, you must never do this again. You must never talk to or hurt another girl. You must never do that Adrian, it is bad." Jocasta didn't feel her words were sufficient but she just didn't have the vocabulary to voice the disgust she felt inside her.

"Adrian you must get rid of your computer and the magazine and you must get rid of these." She picked up the underwear from the table, started to hand it to Adrian but then thought better of it. She didn't want to tempt Adrian with the very things she wanted rid of. "Don't worry, I will do that." She said, putting them into her own pocket.

Adrian stood and embraced his mother. "Thanks mum, I knew you would understand. I will get rid of the computer, I promise. With your help I can get better, I know I can. I love you mum."

"Ok, go to your room now Adrian, I need to clean up the dinner things."

Adrian walked towards his room. "I love you mum." He said again.

"I know," said Jocasta. She could not bring herself to reciprocate Adrian's gesture at that time. She knew that she did love him; loved him like any mother loves a son, but she was still fighting the sickening images in her mind and hate was grappling with the love she had for him. She watched him go to his bedroom and then cleaned up the dinner stuff and sat to watch television. Jocasta looked at the TV but did not see the images; instead she planned just how she was going to get her son off the streets and away from doing any further harm. She hoped and prayed that she had the strength to fulfil the new destiny motherhood had bestowed upon her.

Mother Be The Judge

Chapter 21

'When there are too many policemen there is no liberty. When there are too many soldiers there is no peace. Where there are too many lawyers there is no justice.'

Lyn Yutang

20th May 2012

"Strike," Detective Inspector Todd 'Todger' Turnbull threw his arms into the air in triumph. It was his third strike in the Metropolitan Police Ten Pin Bowling Tournament.

"Well done Guv." Said Detective Sergeant Mary Webb; she patted him on the back as he returned to the circle of chairs around the score keeping console.

"Right, Mary, you try and get more than three pins down now and we might actually win this match."

"Oh it's *my* fault we always lose is it?" Mary rolled her eyes. "That's the first lot of strikes you've had in six matches."

Todd laughed, "Well at least I knock some down."

Mary gave Todd the finger before she turned to roll her ball. She lined up the ball with the arrow on the floor, took a big step forward swinging her right arm back and promptly dropped the ball behind her. It rolled, its glittering surface sparkling before coming to a rest at Todd's feet. He lifted an eyebrow at Mary, then retrieved the bowling ball and passed it back to her.

"Don't say anything." She warned him. Todd laughed again then clapped loudly.

"Come on Mary, let's go," he cheered her on. She eventually managed eight pins followed by a spare, causing Olinsbury's team to win a sweet victory against the rest of the Met.

Todd gave Mary a huge bear hug, congratulating her on her achievement. "Come on Mary," he said, "I'll get you a McDonalds, my treat."

"Big spender," she pushed into him fondly, enjoying his attention. Todd knew she had a not so secret crush on him, but kept their relationship strictly platonic. He did, however, enjoy her company and made sure he never missed their team commitments in the ten pin bowling tournaments.

Todd and Mary left the bowling alley which was near to Heathrow Airport and began to make their way back to Olinsbury police station. They were on night shifts which started at 10pm and the time was drawing near. Todd drove them both in his own car; a silver Vauxhall Cavalier. He knew it was nothing spectacular but it was a reliable and economical car which served the purpose he needed it for. He would buy his bachelor sport's car when he retired. They stopped at McDonalds and Todd ordered his standard meal of quarter pounder with cheese. He didn't particularly like

Mother Be The Judge

this meal, but time had taught him this was the burger which was always ready to go and he would rather have the lukewarm taste of a half decent burger than wait the extra five minutes for something else to be cooked. Time meant everything when crime was your business and Todd made sure he didn't waste any of his.

The station appeared in front of them at the end of Montague Road in Olinsbury.

"Another night in paradise," joked Todd.

"Olinsbury is the new Hollywood," was Mary's standard reply.

"I wonder what the lovely residents have got for us tonight." Todd pressed the button on the security gate and waited to be let into the yard. He made a point of parking in the space reserved for the Borough Commander; as it was the night shift Todd knew there would be no sign of senior management and always took pleasure in taking over their parking spot. It was the little things in life which gave him pleasure. They left the car and buzzed the rear door, wading through the discarded cigarette butts which had been thrown at the outside ashtray by the army of smokers that frequented the back step through the day.

Todd took the lead and went up the stairs to the first floor CID department. He walked through the office offering hellos and exchanging comments with the officers who had either just arrived or who were just leaving, then went into his own office, Mary still following. He sat at his desk and asked Mary to shut the door behind them.

"Right Mary, I want to first go through today's

work and then I want to go over our cold cases." He picked up a sheet of crime reference numbers which the previous shift's Inspector had left for him. Sitting at the Crime Reporting Information System or CRIS for short, Todd brought up each individual crime which had been reported that day.

"Deception, Demanding Money with Menaces, Grievous Bodily Harm," Todd reeled off the crimes to Mary who nodded her head. These crimes were standard to them, reported on a daily basis, no longer shocking to the people who dealt in the business of investigation. Todd continued, "Three burglaries, two rapes."

"And a partridge in a pear tree," sang Mary. Todd grinned and spent a few minutes tapping buttons on the keyboard in front of him, then turned away from the computer screen.

"Yeah, they're all being dealt with," he said, "Nothing we need to do with them." He stood up and went to the shelves at the rear of his office to retrieve two boxes which sat gathering dust. Picking up the first box, he passed it over to Mary who put the box on the desk. Todd then brought the other one over. "These two cases are from 2008, 2009; so nearly four years old."

"Well they're three years old Guv." said Mary, "Let's not make it too bad." Mary hated it when people did that; being conscious of her ever increasing age, she would prefer it if people focused on her being thirty nine rather than increasing it to forty, just because it was near.

"Yes ok, three years." Todd knew Mary's view on this and had actually made the mistake on purpose just to wind her up. He was very aware it had actually been three years, five months and twenty one days since the first crime in the box on the table had occurred. He knew the box contained the file on Savannah West. Todd had a large amount of guilt on his shoulders because he had not been able to catch the person who had lured Savannah to her death. He had not been able to give closure to Savannah's family or to obtain justice in a court of law which would offer a small recompense to them. He still saw visions of Savannah's limp, grey body on the bank of the stream, still recalled the contents of the Coroner's report and the vivid images of depravity it projected. He still suspected that the young man who had found the girl was in some way responsible for Savannah's death; his was the only DNA on her body and although the mother had given him an alibi, Todd was convinced that Adrian Brown was the perpetrator who took Savannah's life in such a brutal way.

The Crown Prosecution Service required evidence beyond reasonable doubt before they would consider prosecuting anybody and whilst Todd knew this was important in the hunt for justice, he was annoyed that it also provided a loophole for defence barristers to play with. The fact that Adrian had held Savannah when he had found her in the stream, gave him the reasonable explanation for why the DNA was there and stopped any chance of a prosecution against him. It wasn't enough to suspect or even to *know* that

Adrian Brown was the killer, if Todd couldn't prove it then the suspicion meant nothing.

Todd took all the paperwork out of the box and started to separate the different documents onto the table. Statements, taped interviews, autopsy reports, search records, pocket book enquiries, missing person reports and then his own notes of people he had spoken to at the time. Both Todd and Mary spent the next hour and a half reading through every piece of paperwork. They knew that often things were missed or misread during investigations; not because of malpractice but it was human nature not to be perfect. A new eye on an investigation or revisiting an old file could often bring a new take on an investigation or offer a previously unnoticed piece of evidence. Today was not going to be that day however, no matter how often Todd read through this file, nothing new came to light; once again the only conclusion he could come to was that the perpetrator was Adrian Brown.

"He will do it again you know." Todd commented to Mary. "A person who does this always strikes again eventually, might have done it already."

"True," agreed Mary, "It's been a while though; it could have been an accident.

Todd guffawed, "You don't accidentally shag an eleven year old Mary, come on."

Mary shrugged, "Alright but it has been three years; he could be dead or may have moved away."

"No he's still here." Said Todd, "I know its Adrian Brown, I know he did it. I don't care what his mother says; I just hope he doesn't do it again because no girl

Mother Be The Judge

deserves to go through what that poor child went through. Has he been picked up for anything else since?"

Mary flicked through the paperwork in front of her. "No Guv. There's just that sexual touching when he was a kid."

Todd sighed and sat back in his chair, it was so frustrating for him to believe he knew someone had committed an offence but to have his hands so tied by rules of evidence that he couldn't bring him to justice.

"Let's keep an eye on missing girls again," he said, "I know we've been lucky lately and not had any go missing for more than twenty four hours, but we still need to make sure we class all of them as High Risk. If a girl goes missing, I want to know about it straight away, especially if she goes missing from the Elisworth area. If a girl goes missing from there I want a full area search immediately."

"Yes Guv." Mary agreed and made a note to include the instruction on the following briefing of officers, both plain clothed and uniformed.

"Right come on hairy Mary; let's look at the next one."

"Oh goody, what have we got?"

Todd lifted the lid on the second box, "Graveyard robberies." He announced.

"Oh I was *dying* to do that one," Mary said.

"Mary that's terrible, stop it or I might die laughing." Todd countered.

They both chuckled and then lost themselves in another hour of reading paperwork.

Chapter 22

'Some mothers are kissing mothers and some are scolding mothers, but it is love just the same and most mothers kiss and scold together.'
Pearl S. Buck

Monday 21st May 2012
08:30 hours

Jocasta arrived at the doctor's surgery in her new work clothes. She felt a bit uncomfortable as the waistband was digging into her stomach. The events of last week had caused her eating to go into overdrive where she constantly tried to keep food in her mind instead of Adrian's evil.

Adrian had been true to his word and had removed the computer from the house. He smashed it up in front of her and put it in a black bag along with the magazine which he ripped up. Jocasta had disposed of Savannah's underwear, wrapping them in kitchen roll and stuffing them at the bottom of the bin bag which she put down the rubbish chute of their flat.

Although Adrian had honoured his promise, Jocasta knew it could not be that simple. When somebody was evil and had lusts, they could not just be switched off. Jocasta had made up her mind that she was going to find a way to keep Adrian at home. Whilst in the doctor's surgery Jocasta would have access to medical books, doctor's notes and prescription paperwork. She intended on researching everything she could on a drug which would replicate the symptoms of M.E. as she knew this was an illness which caused the patient to feel tired all the time and unable to move. Jocasta felt if she could keep Adrian in this frame of mind then he would become housebound and she would be able to protect any further girls from getting hurt.

"Jocasta; hi," Mable, the head receptionist greeted her at the door of the surgery.

"Hi," said Jocasta and held out her hand in greeting. Mable shook her hand but her smile didn't reach her eyes as she took in Jocasta's appearance. Jocasta knew she wasn't the prettiest woman in the world but she was clean and presentable, she objected to the way Mable was looking at her. She hadn't expected a middle-aged woman like Mable to be bothered with a person's appearance.

"Is there a problem?" Jocasta asked, breaking Mable's gaze.

"No, no, sorry Jocasta, I was just admiring your top. It's very pretty." Mable said, the smile now showing in her eyes. This took Jocasta by surprise and she silently scolded herself for jumping to the worst conclusion so readily. She *had* been right, Mable wasn't interested in looks; she had just liked the top Jocasta was wearing. Jocasta realised it was the first compliment that had been paid to her in a very long time. She felt her self-confidence grow and pulled back her shoulders so she could show off her top in full effect, it *was* very pretty; navy blue with little white stars dotted about the flowing material.

"Thank you very much," Jocasta said, "I got it in Primani."

"Well its lovely, come on then let's get you started. If you wouldn't mind filing the medical notes for now, that would be great." Mable led Jocasta to the rear of the surgery and took her into a dingy room lined with shelves which seemed to contain thousands of paper files, stuffed into every available space. Mable pointed to a small wire trolley containing more of the files, piled haphazardly on top of each other.

"It's an easy system." Mable advised Jocasta, "This number is our starting point," she pointed to a number in the top right hand corner of the file; "We then look for the alphabetical surname in the corresponding numbered shelf. Come with me, I'll do the first few for you and then you can get on with it."

Mable picked up the first file, hurried over to a shelf, flicked deftly through the files there and stuffed the new file in amongst the papers. Jocasta didn't see exactly how or where the file had disappeared to and was about to ask for another demonstration when Mable stated, "So that's it, it's easy. I have to go on reception now, let me know when you're finished or if you need any help."

She smiled once again and practically skipped out of the room, obviously happy to leave the mun-

Mother Be The Judge

dane task to somebody else; leaving Jocasta in the middle of shelves, papers and files with no real idea of what she was doing. Jocasta gave a sigh and picked up the nearest file to her on the trolley. At least keeping busy would take her mind off her problems, there didn't seem to be any time limit to the task so Jocasta resolved to take her time and do the job well. The first file was number fifty so Jocasta found the corresponding shelf and began the working day.

* * *

12:30 hours

After nearly four hours of working hard, Jocasta felt ready for lunch. Her thighs were hurting where she had squatted many times to reach the bottom shelves. She had to walk slowly to try and stop the burn and wondered how she would ever be able to finish her day if she was forced to return to filing once her lunch was over.

"Jocasta, would you like to join us for lunch?" Mable called to her as she left the filing room. The offer made Jocasta nervous; she was unaccustomed to company and was concerned she may say or do the wrong thing and spoil her chances of friendship. She retrieved the packed lunch she had made for herself and went to sit at the staff table where Mable already sat with the two other staff. They introduced themselves to her as Karen and Leanne.

Karen was another middle aged lady; Jocasta guessed about fifty years old. She told Jocasta all about her new granddaughter, showing her pictures of a chubby little baby with a shock of blonde hair. Jocasta made all the right noises and actually had a physical pang of desire for a grandchild of her own. Karen seemed pleased with Jocasta's responses and sat back to look at her own photos again; obviously wishing she was at home with her granddaughter instead of at work.

Leanne took over the conversation; she was a much younger woman, only twenty years old. She was only using the doctor's surgery as a stop-gap whilst she waited to bag herself a footballer. Leanne looked like a typical W.A.G; big blonde hair, five layers of makeup, stinking of perfume and eyelashes three times longer than they should be. She regaled them with tales of her night clubbing exploits and how she had almost managed to speak to a footballer who was on the Brentford reserve team, but how she had been prevented by going into the V.I.P. area by the bouncer whose advances she had spurned the week before. Although this type of conversation was completely alien to Jocasta, she enjoyed how Leanne spoke with so much enthusiasm and lust for life. Jocasta envied Leanne her age, beauty and ambition.

Mable didn't have much to say about herself, preferring instead to ask Jocasta about her own life. Jocasta gave a very brief account of how she was a single mother with a son and how no, she didn't know where her name came from because she had been in

Mother Be The Judge

care as a child and had never known her parents. She told them Adrian worked in Big Value and threw in a bit about him having a girlfriend as she was desperate to portray him as normal. The three ladies appeared genuinely interested in Jocasta and she thoroughly enjoyed her first real conversation in many years. Jocasta almost forgot the problems she had waiting for her at home, but she could just feel them hovering in the back of her mind, waiting for her to stop and think about them.

"Right, we better get some work done," said Mable. Jocasta's heart sank at the prospect of returning to the dreary filing room. "But no more filing today," smiled Mable almost as if she had read Jocasta's mind. "Now we need to do the photocopying."

Whoop de do Jocasta thought to herself; hardly delighted she was moving from one dull chore to another.

"Don't worry, it won't take long and then I will show you the phone system so you can do the afternoon reception," said Mable, "We all take turns doing the shitty work; you won't have to do any filing or photocopying tomorrow." Jocasta gave a mental cheer of joy then followed Mable to the photocopier. She wondered when she would get the opportunity to start the research she so desperately needed to do.

* * *

Jocasta now sat in place at reception waiting for the afternoon's patients to come and go. She read each patient's file as she pulled it out, looking for any illness akin to M.E. or for anything which would help her discover a medication that would help Adrian. The afternoon was now just full of coughs and colds, however, people looking for medical certification which would get them a week off work and other mundane illnesses, none of which served Jocasta any purpose. She sat and smiled her way through the afternoon but felt scared inside that whilst she sat there Adrian was in the world unchecked, possibly preying on another girl or at the very least, considering it. Jocasta knew she could not afford to waste any time and needed to find something soon which would solve her problem.

Just as the day was coming to an end, a dishevelled male stumbled through the surgery door. He was either sun tanned or incredibly dirty, his hair was grey, shoulder length and greasy and his blue eyes shone out of red bloodshot sockets.

"Is doctor 'ere?" he slurred at Jocasta, his movements were very slow and deliberate and it seemed to take a lot of concentration just to put one foot in front of the other. Eventually he lowered himself into a chair in the waiting room and immediately began to snore, now apparently fast asleep.

Jocasta looked to Mable who was sitting beside her and waited for instructions on what to do next.

"Temazi Terry." Mable said.

"Eh?" Jocasta didn't understand the reference Mable used.

"Temazi Terry." Mable repeated and then chuckled, "He takes Temazepam for his depression." She made air quotation marks around the word 'depression', "He hasn't really got it, he just pretends so he can get the meds. He loves walking around like a zombie."

"Is that what it does to you then?" asked Jocasta.

"Yeah," Mable said, "I think they make you so dopey you forget to be depressed. I shouldn't be mean; I'm sure he *has* got depression, I'm just getting cynical in my old age." She got up and went over to shake Temazi Terry on the shoulder. "Ter-ry," she sang at him, "Ter-ry." He shook his head slowly then opened his eyes.

"Wha?"

"Your appointment is tomorrow Terry." Mable informed him, "You can't see the doctor now."

"Where's my script?" he asked, dragging himself out of his chair.

"You'll get it to-mor-row." Mable spoke slowly so he would take it all in. "Ok Terry? Come back to-mor-row."

"Eh? Ok." He said and stumbled back out of the front door. Jocasta thought she had just discovered the perfect medicine for what she had to do.

* * *

Tuesday 22nd May 2012

Jocasta returned to work the following day and asked Mable to take her through all the different forms used in the office and where they were all kept. Mable was happy to oblige and went through every drawer and filing cabinet with Jocasta, showing her x-ray requests, blood test sheets, etc. Jocasta wanted to shout at Mable to hurry up and show her where the blank prescriptions were but instead nodded with each form and kept her face interested. Finally after what seemed an eternity, Mable showed Jocasta where the blank prescription forms were kept along with the doctor's signature stamp.

"We don't really use these anymore," explained Mable, "These are just kept here in case the computer breaks down. We have the doctor's signature on a stamp so we can get them done for him. But it's very rare so you don't have to worry about remembering where they are. I think we've only used them once since we put them there." Mable replaced the forms in their relevant drawer and moved onto other forms and documents.

Jocasta spent the rest of her day going through the motions of work. At the first opportunity she got, she grabbed a prescription pad and the signature stamp, secreting them in her bag before she was seen. She was certain that her theft would not be discovered if the forms were so rarely used. Jocasta then spent a short while looking up Temazepam in the pharmaceutical brochure, which discussed dosages, side effects etc. She ripped out the page she needed so she could be sure of what she was doing; Jocasta didn't want to make any mistakes and hurt Adrian.

When the end of her working day came, Jocasta bid her new found friends a fond farewell. She was saddened that she would not be returning to the doctor's surgery, but her most important work now lay at home. She had to be sure Adrian was safely ensconced in their flat as her conscience would not allow her to expose any more children to the evil he had inside him.

Before getting home, Jocasta stopped at Big Value; she went into the customer toilets and wrote out a prescription for the Temazepam, enough for a month. She couldn't chance asking for any more than that as Jocasta didn't want to draw any suspicion on herself. She intended to visit chemists through the next day to collect as many tablets as she could hope to get with the prescriptions that she had. Jocasta didn't know what she would do once the tablets ran out; she would cross that bridge when she came to it. She took the prescription to the twenty four hour pharmacy inside Big Value and stood with her heart in mouth, to await the delivery of the tablets. She got bored of waiting and decided to go and pick a strongly flavoured dinner for Adrian that evening, one which would mask the taste of the Temazepam, although she didn't know whether it had any taste to it or not. Wondering around the aisles, she decided on a fish pie; there was so much cream and fish in the dinner she felt sure it would hide any taste one small pill would provide. Eventually she went back to the pharmacy and continued to wait for what seemed a very long time, expecting an accusing hand on her shoulder with every second that ticked by. Finally the cashier began to hand her a large paper bag with a smile.

"Can you just confirm your name and address?" she asked Jocasta.

"Georgina Perkins; 123 Wilmington Crescent," Jocasta repeated the false name and address she had written on the prescription.

"There you go Mrs Perkins."

"It's Miss," Jocasta gave her automatic reply. The cashier gave a look which said, 'Whatever' and handed the bag over. Jocasta took it, turned on her heel and marched out of the store. She knew the hard part was now to come; it was all very well hatching a plan to keep Adrian in his room but he wasn't just going to swallow tablets at her request. She now had to find a way to administer them without him knowing; she hoped the fish pie lived up to her expectations.

Chapter 23

'Often even a whole city suffers from a bad man who sins.'
Hesiod

Wednesday 23rd May 2012

Adrian was due to go to Big Value and would usually be up by 6am to get ready for his shift. Jocasta had ground a Temazepam tablet into Adrian's fish pie the evening before and he had eaten the meal without any complaint. Jocasta was thankful that Adrian was used to her meals never tasting quite right as she had never been a proficient cook and he had learnt early in his life to eat quickly before taste became a factor.

Jocasta waited until 7am before deciding to enter Adrian's room to check on him. She had been debating doing this for the last hour but she had been so frightened she may have killed him that she kept putting it off. Holding her breath as she walked through Adrian's door and hoping she would see the rise and fall of his chest when she got to his bed, Jocasta walked in the room and over to Adrian's bed. Adrian lay spread-eagled on top of his bed covers in just a pair of boxer shorts and a t-shirt. Jocasta looked down on her son of twenty one years; he didn't seem to be moving at all and Jocasta's heart was in her mouth at the thought she may actually have put an end to her son's life. Thankfully she saw a line of dribble escape from Adrian's mouth and his tongue run around his dry lips.

"Adrian." Jocasta put her hand on his shoulder and gave a small nudge. "Adrian, are you getting up for work?"

Adrian didn't respond to Jocasta's query. He turned over and buried his head into his pillow. Jocasta left him in his bed and went back out to the kitchen. She was pleased to know that the tablets had had the desired effect on Adrian; he didn't seem harmed but was obviously very tired and it was not too late for him to go to work. She picked up the telephone and dialled the number for Adrian's manager at Big Value.

"Hello?"

"Yes, hello, I'm Adrian Brown's mother, Jocasta. I'm afraid he won't be coming into work today, he's not well."

"Oh sorry, you need to speak to the manager, hold on I'll get her for you," came the reply. Jocasta waited patiently for another two minutes, listening to an unknown pop tune playing merrily down the phone line.

"Hello?" a female voice came on the phone.

"Yes, hello, I'm Adrian Brown's mother, Jocasta, I'm afraid he won't be in today, he's not well."

"What's the matter with him?"

"Oh he's been vomiting all night; I think he may

have food poisoning." Jocasta said the first thing that came into her mind; it wasn't far off the truth. She didn't think that to say, 'he hasn't got up yet' would be enough to justify him not getting to work.

"Is it self-certified?" enquired the manager. Jocasta noticed the manager did not seem concerned for Adrian and was not showing any regret for Adrian's illness. In fact, the manager seemed very cold and indifferent towards Adrian. Jocasta felt her normal distaste for the way people treated her son.

"Yes it's self-certified. If it becomes more serious then I will take him to the doctors." Jocasta poked her tongue out at the phone receiver hoping to send it along the line to the manager's ear.

"Ok well I suppose I will have to find someone else to do the cold room." The manager sighed. "When is he coming back?"

"I don't know, but when I do then you will know." Jocasta said. She was getting fed up of having this conversation, it should have been over after the first few seconds and she begrudged all the questions when she should be checking on how Adrian was doing. Jocasta started to hop from one foot to another in her frustration at being kept on the phone. The manager sighed again, "Ok well please phone tomorrow if he's not coming in."

"Yes ok, thank you." Jocasta gave the phone two fingers as she replaced the receiver in its cradle. "I hope he is ok." She said the words she expected the manager to have used, but never heard.

As Jocasta sat at the kitchen table eating scrambled eggs on toast, Adrian stumbled into the hallway of their flat.

"Mum." He called out, he held onto the hallway with one hand and his head with the other.

"Mum," he called again. Jocasta got up from her seat at the table and walked to Adrian in the hallway.

"What's the matter?" she asked him.

"I don't feel well." He told her. "My head is spinning. I feel like I need to go back to bed, can you phone work and tell them I won't be in?"

"Yes of course I can, go back to bed and I'll get you an aspirin."

Adrian turned and walked slowly back to his bed, then fell back onto the divan; groaning and rubbing at his forehead. Jocasta went back to the kitchen and broke another Temazepam out of its bubble packet. She poured a glass of water and took the tablet to Adrian.

"Here Adrian, here's an Anadin, take it for your headache."

Adrian pushed himself up into a sitting position and reached out for the cup Jocasta offered him. He swallowed the tablet, finished the water in the cup and then lay back down on the bed. Jocasta retrieved the quilt which was bunched up at the end of the bed and covered Adrian with it. She leant down to kiss him on the forehead. He didn't register the kiss at all and Jocasta felt a pang of guilt that she was the cause of his condition. She left the room and went into the front room, turned on the television and waited for Jeremy Kyle. She wished her problems were so trivial that she could afford to have them broadcast on national television, because she would have loved to have somebody to talk to and get some advice on what to do with Adrian. She could just picture Jeremy's face when she sat in one of the padded chairs on his stage. "Oh yes Jeremy, my son is a paedophile who raped and murdered a little girl and now I have him drugged up in his bedroom." Jocasta didn't think an hour's show would be any way near long enough to sort that kind of mess out. She knew she was on her own and would just have to deal with things the best way that she could. Remembering that she still had to visit different chemists to pick up further Temazepam prescriptions, Jocasta got up to take a shower and get dressed. She figured she had a good four hours, maybe more, before Adrian would wake up again which should be enough time to get around Elisworth and pick up the prescriptions and some ingredients for the soup she was hoping to secrete Adrian's next dosage in. He had taken the Anadin so readily however, she knew that it was not going to be a problem giving him any further doses, so long as he didn't realise that it wasn't Anadin she was giving him.

* * *

Jocasta quickly checked Adrian was still sleeping before she let herself quietly out of their flat. She walked briskly down the communal steps and out into the children's playground.

A young boy, no more than ten years old, sat on the bench; balancing on the two remaining wooden slats of the seat. Slumped over next to him was a body; Jocasta couldn't see if it was male or female as the dark grey clothing being worn was sports like; track-suit bottoms with dirty white trainers and a hooded top which obscured any hair or facial features. The person's head was also hidden behind where the boy sat on the bench. Jocasta only meant to give the couple a fleeting glimpse as she wasn't nosy and was too wrapped up in her own problems to worry about anyone else's, but her glimpse triggered recognition and she stopped to look at the young boy properly.

The boy was looking despondently at the floor. Jocasta recognised the mousy brown hair and skeletal features of Andrew West. She supposed the slumped being behind him must be Mae, Savannah's mother, as she knew that the step-father Mike was no longer on the scene. Jocasta felt a pang of deep remorse that her son could have reduced this woman to being passed out in a children's playground. She was very aware that if Savannah were alive it was highly possible that Mae West would be passed out at home on the sofa as she was an alcoholic *before* Savannah died, however, being unconscious outside left Mae open to reports of neglect and would court attention from the Social Security. Jocasta didn't think she would be able to live with herself if Mae lost her second child, albeit he would be better looked after. Rather than walk away as would have been her usual behaviour, Jocasta decided to stop and help as she felt she had a responsibility now to care for this family; the victims of her son's evil, the people who were left behind to face the pain of losing their family member.

"Hello, its Andrew isn't it?" Jocasta approached the lad. He gave her a dirty look and shrank back into his mother's body.

"It's ok, I live up there." Jocasta gestured to her flat above. "Is that your mum?"

Andrew gave a nod. "She won't wake up," he said. Jocasta heard a grumbling coming from the boy's stomach. It was only 8 o'clock in the morning. Jocasta realised it was very possible that Andrew had been sitting with his mother throughout the night. She was glad that at least the weather was mild or Andrew might not have been so alive when she found him. He may not only be suffering from hunger, but exposure as well.

"Have you been here all night?" She asked him.

"Yeah, she won't wake up." Andrew gave the same reply.

Fearing that Mae may actually be dead, Jocasta rushed over to her slumped figure and gave Mae a push on the shoulder, bringing Mae's face into view. Mae's lips were blue but her face still had what Jocasta considered an 'alive' look about it. She shook Mae harder and shouted at her to wake up.

Mae opened her bloodshot eyes and looked up at Jocasta.

"What do you want? Fuck off." She shouted at Jocasta.

"It's Mae isn't it?" Jocasta asked her.

"What the fuck has that got to do with you?" Mae was obviously extremely annoyed at being disturbed from her drunken stupor. And drunk she was; she stank of stale alcohol, urine and vomit. Jocasta had to put her hand to her nose to shield herself from the smell Mae was giving off.

"Mae, you can't lie out here, if the police see you they'll phone the Social Services." Jocasta pleaded with her. She was hoping the threat of the Social would spur Mae into action.

"Fuck the police. They didn't help me, I'm staying here. Sav loved it here." Mae reached out and put her arms around Andrew, pulling him nearer to her and burying her head in his lap.

"My Sav loved this playground." She wailed and then began to cry in earnest.

Andrew looked pleadingly at Jocasta; she knew he must be cold, hungry and very tired. She could easily have walked away, but Jocasta was determined to help Mae and Andrew. She took Andrew's hand and extricated him from his mother's grip. Then sat where he had been sitting and put her arm around Mae's shoulders. "Come on Mae, let's get you home."

Mae continued to cry but despair had made her weak and she allowed herself to be manoeuvred off the bench by Jocasta. Mae stood up, but wobbled violently, so Jocasta put her arm around her and allowed Mae to lean heavily on her, then she led the way to where she knew Mae and Andrew lived. Andrew followed behind, kicking an empty beer can before him; one of many which had been discarded on the playground floor, next to food wrappers, an empty syringe and a large pile of dried up dog poo.

It was a short but arduous walk back to Mae's flat as Mae found it very difficult to put one foot in front of the other. Jocasta was sure Mae had ingested more than just alcohol; there was no way alcohol could have caused such huge impairment, especially as Mae had apparently been asleep for some time. Jocasta helped Mae through her front door, after she had spent a few minutes fumbling through Mae's pockets for the front door keys, only to be told that the key was under the door mat. Andrew retrieved it for Jocasta who then opened the door.

When Jocasta entered the flat, she found it in a terrible state. Rubbish, mainly empty and crushed beer cans, pizza boxes and dirty clothes, was scattered everywhere. It was difficult to find an empty patch of floor to put a foot in. Jocasta didn't think that Mae had cleaned or tidied the flat for a very long time; she obviously wasn't coping with the loss of her daughter. Andrew ran to the kitchen and returned; an embarrassed look on his face, with a roll of black bags which he handed to Jocasta.

"Is there any food in the house?" Jocasta asked him, he shrugged but looked hopeful at the prospect of food.

Jocasta led Mae to her bedroom, led by Andrew and helped Mae into her sheet-less bed. She found a blanket bunched up in the corner of the room and then went to the kitchen to find something for Andrew to eat, coming up with a box of cereal and some dubious milk. Andrew scoffed the food very quickly obviously glad for anything which he could put in his belly.

Jocasta picked up all the rubbish and Andrew showed her where everything was in the flat. There were no cleaning products to speak of so Jocasta made do with a bucket of warm water and a raggedy old dishcloth that had been in the sink. She worked hard for two hours, cleaning and making things right. When she entered Andrew's bedroom, Jocasta found Savannah's bed and belongings in immaculate condition. The bed was made and a small teddy bear sat propped up on the pillow. It was a grey bear with blue patches on it and was holding a banner saying 'Daughter', Photos of Savannah were stuck on the wall around the headboard; Savannah at the beach, school pictures and photo booth pictures of Savannah with her friends. Jocasta recognised Lacey in a couple of the pictures. They were happy photos, capturing moments in Savannah's life where she was growing up and experiencing new things. Jocasta was sad that there would never be a picture of Savannah as a grown woman, getting married, holding a child or grandchildren. No camera would ever capture Savannah's face again.

Andrew watched Jocasta as she looked at Savannah's belongings. He hadn't spoken but she could tell that he was guarding the property, making sure Jocasta didn't touch his sister's precious memories.

"You miss her don't you?" Jocasta said. Andrew nodded and tears welled up in his eyes. He went to sit on his own bed, turning on the television and losing himself in SpongeBob Square pants; dismissing

Jocasta from his attention. Jocasta left the room, she wanted to scoop Andrew up into her arms and tell him everything was going to be ok, but it wasn't and it never would be. Adrian had not just taken Savannah's life; he had taken the life of Andrew and the life of Mae also. Even if time did eventually heal their emotional wounds, neither Andrew nor Mae's life would ever be the same again. Mae had obviously pressed the self-destruct button and Jocasta knew it wouldn't be long before Andrew followed suit, influenced by the life he watched his mother lead. She made a promise to herself that she would keep an eye on the Wests and would help them out whenever she could. Maybe in some small way she would be able to help them to recover from their terrible loss.

Jocasta left the flat and made her way to the first on the list of Chemists she had to visit that day; now more determined than ever to keep Adrian at home and unable to cause any more harm to a living creature.

Chapter 24

'God places the heaviest burden on those who can carry its weight.'
   Reggie White

Jocasta stayed out for a lot longer then she had expected, her chance meeting with Mae and Andrew had taken a good two hours of her time and every chemist was about twenty minutes away from the next one. Add to that the waiting time and Jocasta had only managed to visit two chemists before realising she could do no more. It was imperative she kept Adrian under the influence of the Temazepam because even though she was certain Adrian would not suspect her of any wrongdoing; if Adrian was able to recover and was then re-drugged, Jocasta knew it was likely he would become suspicious. If Adrian began to refuse her cooking or medication she offered him, then Jocasta would have no means of keeping him home and in her mind that wasn't an option.

Still with the vision of Savannah's protected belongings on her mind, Jocasta went home and made a tomato soup. She didn't make it from scratch, her cooking skills were basic and soup was way out of her comfort zone. She stood and watched the soup bubbling, feeling quite hungry herself after all the walking and lying she had been doing. As the red bubbles popped and splattered, Jocasta had an overwhelming urge to take her own life. She imagined jumping into a big vat of burning soup and allowing the heat to envelope her, causing her to melt away along with all her problems. She hoped reincarnation was real; she would come back as a giant land tortoise and live a long, slow, pain free life; chewing on lettuce and occasionally humping rocks.

A sound from the hallway broke Jocasta out of her daydreaming; she turned to see Adrian stumbling down the hallway.

"Hello love, are you feeling better?" Jocasta asked him.

"Not really." Adrian said, "It's like I can't wake up."

"Sleep is the best thing when you're sick." Jocasta turned back to tend to the soup. "It's your body's way of healing itself." She told him.

"Yeah," Adrian agreed as he sat at the table, struggling to pull the chair out before he could get his rear on the seat. "I can't remember anything that happened yesterday, it's like I've lost a day of my life."

"Oh that's just..." Jocasta stopped herself from saying 'the side effect' as that would surely draw suspicion upon her. She knew then that what she was doing was ridiculous. She wondered how she could possibly keep up the constant dosage of Temazepam which would keep Adrian asleep or dopey enough to not want to leave the flat. She also wondered what would happen once the medicine ran out, but more than anything she felt a terrible guilt for causing harm to her son. As a mother she believed it was her job to protect Adrian from harm and she had tried to do that all of his life. Now she found herself protecting others *from* Adrian; this wasn't how life was supposed to be. She should be proud of Adrian and boasting of his achievements, not hiding him away in their flat, ashamed of what he had become.

"That's just because you've done nothing but sleep." Jocasta reasoned. She spooned the soup into two bowls and broke up some bread on a separate plate, then brought them to the table.

"I'll get you another Anadin." Jocasta told Adrian, "Have you still got a headache?"

"Yeah," Adrian's eyes were half closed as he spoke.

Jocasta went to the cupboard where she kept the Temazepam and broke another one out of its pack. She handed one to Adrian and gave him a glass of water; he took it without question and swallowed the small tablet along with a gulp of water.

Jocasta sat at the table and began to eat her soup.

"I saw Savannah's mother today." She told him. Adrian didn't seem to register the statement.

"She was in a terrible state, her house was a mess and she was almost comatose with drink." Jocasta continued to tell Adrian what had happened. She was aware Adrian was not really listening but she needed to tell someone what had happened. As she spoke, Adrian's head dropped lower and lower, he held his spoon mid-scoop and all motion stopped. Jocasta realised that he had fallen asleep. She shouted his name,

"Adrian."

He gave a slight shake of his head and looked up at her.

"Savannah was sweet." He said and smiled, "I enjoyed Savannah." Then his head dropped again. Jocasta was horrified to see the smile on Adrian's face when he spoke of Savannah. She could see that even in his drugged and confused state he had no remorse for what he had done and even seemed proud. Any misgivings which may have been forming whilst warming the soup quickly left Jocasta's mind. She knew she was doing the right thing, there was no way she could ever allow Adrian to get back out into the world; he was a danger to the young girls who might cross his path. When the medicine ran out, she decided, she would go to the doctors herself and pretend the symptoms of depression. Any medication she may be prescribed would go towards her efforts at restraining Adrian. Jocasta's heart was heavy at the prospect of the life which lay before her; a gatekeeper to a world of evil. The lamp that contained Aladdin's genie except this genie was evil and would be in no mood for granting wishes if he was ever set free from his living prison.

Chapter 25

'A mother understands what her child does not say.'
Jewish proverb

24ᵗʰ May 2012
13:00 hours

"Arthur, we *have* to go to the police." Tiffany's mother, Susan, pleaded with her husband. "We haven't heard from her for two days.

Susan and Arthur sat in their front room. The room was immaculately furnished in IKEA flat-pack furniture; the effect was a plain but modern living environment. Susan had spent two years furnishing their home, putting a lot of effort into every detail, adding knick knacks and ornaments to every available space in an attempt to put her own stamp on the generic furniture. Photos of Tiffany adorned the sideboard and she smiled down at them as they sat on the sofa discussing where they might be.

"Her phone may have run out of battery." Arthur said to Susan. "Or she might just not want to talk to us anymore." Arthur ran a hand through his dishevelled hair. He looked extremely rumpled and out of place in such a tidy room. Susan was similarly dishevelled, neither parent being able to concentrate on personal hygiene or appearance when they were so worried about their missing daughter.

"Arthur, the police will help us. She is missing; we haven't seen her for *eight* days. It doesn't matter that she's been texting; that might not even be her."

Arthur looked at Susan, she had voiced a fear he had been harbouring but had not voiced for fear of making it true. "I know." His voice wavered as the emotion bubbled up inside him. "I know, I know, she could be..." his voice broke off; he couldn't bring himself to say aloud his darkest thought.

"Dead," Susan said it for him, "She could be dead."

Arthur reached for Susan and she crumpled into his embrace. Their tears mingled as once again their grief poured out. They had sat like this since Tiffany had not come home; confused by her disappearance and unsure of what they could do to convince her to return. Every text they had received had given them hope that Tiffany may be on her way home, only for Tiffany to scupper their hopes of reuniting. She would just say that she was fine, needed some space and would come home when she was ready. Two days ago, however, the texts had abruptly stopped. Susan had sent countless texts to Tiffany's phone since then, begging her for a reply, but to no avail.

Susan pulled herself out of Arthur's embrace. "Well I'm getting ready and I'm going to the police," she told him.

"Yes you're right," Arthur agreed, "We have to do something."

Susan and Arthur both went upstairs and showered, brushed their teeth and put on some smart clothes; even in grief their sense of self-respect would not allow them to go into the world looking unkempt. They left the house, setting the burglar alarm in their habitual way, then got into the family saloon and made their way to the police station.

* * *

14:00 hours

PC Tom Hunter was back in the station office. It was unusually quiet for two in the afternoon and Tom allowed his mind to ponder his situation at work. When he had joined the police force or 'service' as he had been conditioned to think of it, he had been certain that he was going to change the world. He had been a popular lad at school but found academia was not his strong point. Barely scraping through his exams, Tom had wondered where to go with his life as any notion of becoming a solicitor went out of the window when a series of D's were typed onto his grade sheets. Tom had decided the next best thing was to be a police officer; he was physically fit and able to answer basic maths and English tests. The money was good and he would be respected by his family and the community for following a path of righteousness rather than resorting to crime in order to line his pockets.

When he finally - two attempts at applying later - was welcomed into the service, he enjoyed his training and settled in well amongst like-minded individuals. When Tom left Hendon police training school, he was filled with a sense of power and with a determination to be the best thief taker the Met could spend its money on.

Reality was never as successful as imagination and Tom found that rather than becoming a Super Hero, fighting bad and saving the world, he had become a very small cog in a badly oiled machine which was wrapped very securely in reams of red tape. More often than not evil triumphed over good and justice was just a word saved for films and dreamers. Tom had begun his career keen, willing to believe a victim's story and sure that he would bring all criminals to justice. Since he had started as a police officer, he had been lied to countless times by victims and suspects alike, he had seen pathetic sentences handed out by Magistrates unwilling or frightened to use the full power of the law and had also watched smug criminals walk free from the court because either the Crown Prosecution Service had failed to build a case successfully or because the defence had managed to convince a jury there was a reasonable doubt. Now Tom just went through the daily motions of his role. He hadn't bothered to seek promotion or change into a detective; he enjoyed the camaraderie of his team and his ambition had been lost along with any hopes of becoming a solicitor. Every story he was given by victims was no longer met with belief and a desire to help but with cynicism and a desire to deflect any responsibility for investigations. Tom often offered to take the Station Officer role, it meant he could earn his money with no real threat of personal danger, would more than likely finish his shift when expected and would have access to as many teas and cheese sandwiches as his expanding waistline could handle.

The front door of the police station creaked open and Tom saw a middle aged, respectable looking couple walk into the reception area. Out of habit Tom looked the couple over and made a quick assessment of who they may be or what they could possible desire from the police. Tom decided the couple were married and their clothing suggested they were working class at the very least. He noticed the couples faces were not in keeping with their clothes; they both had heavy bags under tear laden eyes. He quickly assessed this was not someone producing documents; this couple had experienced something upsetting and needed a sympathetic ear rather than an officious policeman. Slipping easily into the role, Tom smiled kindly at the couple and began his investigation.

"Hello," he said. The couple offered reserved smiles. "How can I help you?" he enquired.

"It's our daughter," Arthur began, "She's run away."

"Ok," said Tom. "Come around to the other counter and I will take a report from you."

Arthur gave a sigh of relief. He had expected to be sent away and told there was nothing which could be done, but he was relieved to find a policeman who seemed willing to listen to their story and hopefully help them to get their daughter back.

Tom spent the next hour with Arthur and Susan, getting a full story of Tiffany's disappearance. He filled out a missing person's report and took a full description of Tiffany. Tom was now always mindful of Savannah West; when he had reported her missing his cynical mind had meant he did not put as much effort into the report as he should have done. When her body had been found, it was a stark reminder to him that for every hundred false or resolved reports there was always a possibility that one report would result in a dead child. Tom always ensured from that day on that he took every missing report seriously as he never wanted to feel the guilt he had felt at Savannah's death again.

Reassuring Arthur and Susan that the police would do everything they could to help them find Tiffany, Tom sent them home and asked them to wait for an officer to do the customary house search. He pressed the button on the computer which would send the missing person report to all concerned parties and then went to the control room to circulate Tiffany's description and to ask a police officer to visit the parent's address. Tom just hoped that this would be another girl found at a friend's, hiding from life and her parents. He hoped the police would be able to reunite the family and they could carry on their lives, resolving their problems. More than anything he hoped he was not once again the first point of contact to the parents of a murdered child.

* * *

Detective Inspector Todd 'Todger' Turnbull was sitting at his desk pouring over a two hundred and fifty six paged bank statement. He was investigating a bank's cashier who had been syphoning pennies off customer's bank accounts; amounts so small they would not arouse suspicion of theft. A yearly audit by an astute auditor however, had uncovered the theft and Todd was knee-deep in paperwork and bank manager.

He was grateful for the knock at his door which gave him an excuse to break away from the monotony of financial investigation. "Come in," he shouted and looked up to see Detective Sergeant Mary Webb come in the room.

"Ah here she is to brighten up my day." Todd said. Mary blushed, but got straight down to business.

"Just had a girl reported missing Guv."

"Talk to me." Todd said, dropping his pen on the desk and leaning back in his chair.

"Eleven year old girl; Tiffany Jones, she's been missing since the 16th May."

"What?" Todd sat upright, "Why have they taken so long to report her as missing?"

Mary held up a hand in supplication, "Wait Guv,

hold on." Todd sat back again; he couldn't believe there was *any* good reason for parent's waiting *eight* days before reporting their eleven year old child missing.

"She's been texting them Guv." Mary said, "On the day she didn't come home, she text them to say she wasn't coming back."

"But she's *eleven*." Todd was incredulous that the parents had just seemed to accept the child's text without making an effort to find her. He was aware that people never behaved in the way others considered correct. Thought patterns and circumstance often changed the way people behaved and it was not uncommon for victims to go to the police as a last resort instead of the first option, for fear of appearing weak or because they didn't want to air their dirty laundry in public.

"I know Guv." Mary flicked through the papers she held. "They have been texting her and she was replying, so they didn't think the police would be interested."

"So why have they reported it now?" He asked her.

"Well she stopped texting." Mary shrugged, "They haven't heard from her for two days. She's not replied to any texts or made any contact with them whatsoever. They came this morning; we've already sent an officer around to search their house."

"Ok so we've got an eleven year old who hasn't been seen for eight days and apparently had no contact for the last two." Todd knew the messages meant nothing. History had shown that mobile phones were often used by criminals to throw police off the scent and to twist the truth. Todd had a growing sense of realisation that Tiffany Jones could very well be the newest victim of the unknown killer of Savannah West. Or the victim of Adrian Brown if *his* suspicions were correct.

"Right Mary, you know what I want you to do, get a search going."

"Yes Guv."

"I want *everywhere* searched, starting with Elisworth's parks and definitely the allotments and that stream where Savannah West was found."

"Yes Guv. I've already called in the spare team."

"And ring the dog section," Todd added, "Do they have a cadaver dog yet?" Todd knew that there were now dogs trained to detect rotting flesh.

"They've got one, but it's based in North London." Mary said.

"I don't care if it's based in fucking Scotland, get it down here," said Todd. He knew that as Tiffany had been missing for probably eight days; they were more than likely looking for a corpse rather than a living, breathing child. Tiffany was cold, dead and alone somewhere waiting for Todd to find her and reunite her with her grieving parents.

Chapter 26

'Ignorance is bliss.'
Thomas Gray

24ᵗʰ May 2012
16:00 hours

Adrian had been asleep or in a stupor for the last three days. He was starting to come around again after another long sleep. Adrian felt very hazy in his mind and again couldn't recall much of what had happened during the days he had been ill, he knew his mother had stayed home from work to look after him and was grateful that she had as he probably wouldn't have been able to eat or drink anything without her help. Nothing in Adrian made him suspect his mother of any wrongdoing; he believed in his powers of manipulation and was certain he still had his mother under his spell.

Adrian briefly considered Tiffany's phone, he had kept up a constant communication with her parents and was enjoying the feeling of power he held over the desperate couple. He was unsure how long it had been since he had last text them but the unknown medication coursing through his veins caused him to no longer care. He looked at the table beside his bed and saw the Anadin and a glass of water his mother had left for him. Hoping it would finally cure his befuddled head; he took the Anadin and settled himself back into his bedclothes. The happy side effect for Adrian was that he was having very vivid recollections of his time with Savannah and Tiffany; he was quite enjoying his mystery illness so was in no rush to leave the comfort of his bed.

* * *

Jocasta sat on her brown sofa. She had moved seats a year ago as her usual position had sunk so much she couldn't shift herself out of it without great effort. She was watching Deal or No Deal and was momentarily relieved of her problems as she shouted at the television, "No Deal you plum," whilst one of Britain's finest decided whether to gamble £2,000 on the opening of a box. Jocasta had visited all the chemists on her list today and now had a stockpile of tablets which would keep Adrian in his room for at least the next year. Knowing that keeping Adrian at home meant no further child would suffer at his hands, was a comfort to Jocasta. She was accustomed to spending time alone at home and used to her own company so had no problem consigning herself to this self-imposed prison.

Jocasta hoped that eventually she would be able

Mother Be The Judge

to speak to Adrian about his warped sexual proclivity and in some way help to cure him of his evil desires. She had seen a documentary about conversion therapy. It stated that a guy called Sigmund Freud believed that hypnotic suggestion could turn a homosexual's way of thinking from gay to straight. Jocasta was hopeful that the same thing may be achieved with Adrian if she was to talk through his problems and maybe convince him to seek hypnotherapy. Maybe in the next few months she may get back the beautiful, sweet child that she had raised and bury the vile evil monster that was cuckooing its evil thoughts in Adrian's brain.

Jocasta laughed at the telly as the contestant on the television show lost £5,000 opening the final box and finding themselves the new owner of a shiny penny. She wondered if the contestants were actually given a penny or whether it was all for show. She reached for the box of Just Brazils which sat invitingly on the table before her, then sat back to enjoy the crunch of nut and the warmth of the chocolate whilst she continued to watch the television.

Chapter 27

'I do not seek, I find.'
Pablo Picasso

24ᵗʰ May 2012
17:00 hours

The search team was up and running. It had taken a little while for Detective Sergeant Mary Webb to put together a summary of Tiffany's last known movements, her description and friends - which weren't many - and then to disseminate the information to police officers already on duty and to the spare team who had been called away from the training schedule they would ordinarily keep on a day their shift was not operational.

The cadaver dog was due to enter the Olinsbury borough at around 18:00 hours with directions to start at the allotments where Savannah West had been found. Detective Inspector Todd 'Todger' Turnbull knew that criminals were creatures of habit and the most likely scenario if Tiffany's killer was the same person; was that she may be found in the stream where Savannah had been. Todd hoped that Tiffany was a genuine runaway and that she really was just hiding away from the world but he wasn't going to leave her lying dead somewhere if that had in fact been her fate.

At such short notice it wasn't possible to accrue a team larger than thirty officers, so Todd made sure they were concentrated on the area surrounding Tiffany's school, working their way through Elisworth and checking all known public spaces and parks. The search would take a long time as there was much land to cover. Todd knew that it would probably prove a fruitless exercise; in a town like Elisworth there were few areas of land which remained continuously empty. Parks and recreational areas were often visited by parents with their children, joggers, dog walkers and local drunks looking for somewhere to imbibe away from the eyes of the law. Todd felt sure that if a dead body had been dumped in any of these places then it would have quickly been discovered. He continued with dispersing the teams to these areas, however, as he didn't want to make any mistakes in the hunt for Tiffany.

* * *

Todd made his way to the allotments; he wanted to take control of the search party there as a gut feeling was drawing him back to where Savannah had died. He parked up his Vauxhall in the muddy alleyway and got out of his car, stepping into a grey and rainy day.

Pulling up the hood on his anorak, he made his way to the gates where a group of four officers stood in their blue police issue jumpsuits which were used for the purposes of searching.

"Lovely day Guv," One of the officers Todd knew as Navdeep called out to him.

"I know," Todd replied, "It's supposed to be summer for fucks sake." Todd liked to speak to the officers on their level. He didn't use his elevated rank as a badge of honour which granted him the right to a certain kind of snobbery he had seen displayed by other like-ranked officers. Instead Todd considered himself a police officer first and foremost and the officers knew and respected this.

"Yeah, going to be like it until July," Navdeep said. Todd marvelled at how in any given situation the British were *always* able to discuss the weather. He watched as the other three officers gave murmurs of disappointment; it was bad enough they were doing such a difficult job without adding rain into the mix.

"Do you think the dog will be able to smell anything in this weather?" enquired another officer. Todd hadn't considered that rain may be a factor in smell and he felt a little forlorn at the prospect.

"Well that's why you lot are here," grinned Todd. "That's what hands and knees are for gents, get on 'em and get searching."

Todd, sans uniform, got on his own hands and knees just inside the gate of the allotments. The officers lined up next to him on their own knees and the group began to move slowly forward; eyes scanning the ground before them for any clue which may lead them to learn the whereabouts of Tiffany Jones.

* * *

18:00 hours

The dog van arrived just as Todd's right knee sank into a pile of dark black and very smelly faeces.

"Oh for fox sake," Todd exclaimed to the tittering officers alongside him. He looked up to see the white van parking with its rear doors pointing towards the allotment gates. A loud deep bark was coming from the back of the van and Todd felt the rise of anticipation at the prospect of solving the riddle of Tiffany's disappearance. He prepared himself for what was to come as every sense he had developed as a police officer told him that she was somewhere on the allotment and he felt sure the dog was about to show him where.

Todd took out his mobile phone and called DS Mary Webb.

"Mary, the dog is here at the allotment now," he advised her, "Can you get down here and make sure that the SOCO's are ready to go?" he wanted any crime scene locked down as soon as possible as he was determined that nobody would be able to contaminate the scene and possibly prevent him from gaining justice.

"Oh and I need the photographer and a tent here because it's pissing down."

"Have you found her then Guv?" enquired Mary.

"Well no I haven't yet." Todd said, exasperated at the question. "But she's here Mary, I know she is; just get them down here. Oh and bring me a coffee please."

Todd pressed the button to end his call before Mary had a chance to respond to him. He walked over to where the officer from the dog unit was releasing a large German Shepherd from its cage in the back of the van. The dog could only be described as a beast. It was a magnificent example of a German Shepherd with the familiar sloping back and shortened back legged look akin with the bread. It was a very tall dog, its head reaching the hip of the officer who restrained the dog on its leash. A large pink tongue lolled around the dog's mouth and its eyes bulged with excitement. The German Shepherd pulled at the leash, obviously eager to do the job he was trained to do. All twelve stones of the dog put its handler's strength to the test.

"Rocky, pack up," The officer chastised him. The dog settled back and started to pant heavily waiting further instruction.

"Hi," Todd came forward. The dog lunged at Todd and was pulled back by its handler. Todd hadn't flinched; he was used to the energetic enthusiasm of police dogs and had complete faith in its handler's abilities.

"Hello is D.I. Turnbull here?" enquired the officer.

"Yeah, that's me." Todd rubbed his dirty hands down his even dirtier trousers in an attempt to offer a clean hand to shake.

Mother Be The Judge

"Sorry," said Todd, "It's real dirty and wet out here."

"That's alright sir," the officer said, obviously used to these kind of situations. "Where do you want me to start?"

Todd pointed towards the narrow dirt path which led away from the allotments and towards the stream which ran under the dual carriageway that ran above it.

"Can you take him over there first, we found a girl there a few years ago, and it's possible she is over there."

The dog handler looked towards where Todd was pointing and nodded ascent then made his way, dog on leash, to the stream. Todd returned to the search team which by now had reached the square plots of the allotments. He got back into his position in the middle of their line and began once again with his search for clues.

* * *

18:30 hours

Todd was aware of the sound of a car pulling up in the alleyway. Thinking it must be Mary Webb; Todd stood up once again and took a long stretch, shaking out his legs to relieve the pressure on his knees. His team had covered all the plots on the allotment in the pouring rain and the search so far had come to nothing. Todd hoped there would be some news from the cadaver dog soon, but was getting the feeling his police senses may have been wrong.

Instead of Mary appearing at the gates of the allotment, Todd saw that Jogesh Singh a local news reporter; stood in her stead. He grimaced and began to walk towards the reporter noticing the familiar cameraman who always followed him around.

"What are you doing here?" Todd asked him.

Jogesh grinned, "I heard through the grapevine that another girl has gone missing." He said, "Have you found her yet?"

Todd was angry, it annoyed him that someone from the police had had the gall to call the Press. He made a vow to find out who it was and to give them a well-deserved bollocking.

"You know I can't tell you anything." Todd said to him, "You have to wait for a press release or speak to our press office. Now don't come any closer, you will be trespassing on a potential crime scene."

Smelling an exclusive, Jogesh inched closer to where Todd was standing. "So you *have* got a missing child? You should talk to me, we could maybe help you to find her," he offered.

"No," said Todd, "You know the rules; when I've got something to tell you then I will. Now I can't make you leave but you step one foot on this allotment and I will nick you for obstructing a police investigation."

"Alright, don't worry." Jogesh ran his hands through his thick black hair. "We will wait here, Greg, set up the camera." He turned to his cameraman who began to set up a tripod where they were standing, Todd, now seemingly dismissed as they went about their business of snooping for monetary gain.

Todd was always saddened at the way reporters saw any opportunity as a money maker and were probably the only people in the world, apart from the perpetrators, who were excited by death; the more gruesome the better. Everything had its price it seemed and even death and destruction were an opportunity for the vultures that chose to report on it. Todd had actually had a heated debate in the past with a reporter friend over copious amounts of beer. Todd had given the friend his viewpoint and had listened to his friend telling him that reporting the news was a public service and that people had a right to learn what was going on in the world. He had pointed out the many times the Press had exposed wrongdoing and helped to bring people to justice and explained monetary gain was just a happy side effect of being a reporter. His friend maintained that he would be a reporter regardless of the finances as he had a nose for a story and enjoyed a feeling of achievement when he delivered a good report. Todd had grudgingly accepted his friend's explanation and they had both agreed crime and journalism would always go hand in hand. That didn't stop Todd feeling pissed off every time a reporter turned up at one of his investigations.

* * *

The heavy panting heralded the return of Rocky the cadaver dog and his handler. Todd knew the search had been fruitless otherwise it would be him going to them rather them the other way around.

"Nothing?" he asked the question which didn't require an answer.

"It's very wet up there," the handler said, his drenched hair and clothes bearing testament to that. Rocky gave a vigorous shake, pink tongue swinging furiously with every sideways movement of the head.

"Ok," said Todd, "Can you go over the allotment plots?"

"Yes sir, no problem." The handler pulled at Rocky's neck and pointed him in the direction of the plots of land. The handler allowed the dog's leash to get longer and followed Rocky as his nose made its way across the wet terrain.

DS Mary Webb finally arrived in the passenger seat of the Scenes of Crime Officer's van. The alleyway was already chock a block with cars, a dog van and a reporter so she instructed Jan the SOCO to park on the road outside. Mary slipped and slided her way up the dirt path and then went over to the group which had been created by Todd and his search officers. Jan followed, carrying a tray of paper cups holding luke-warm coffee that had been hot when purchased from the coffee shop fifteen minutes earlier.

Mary and Jan were met with low level cheers of approval when the cold and wet officers saw them with their tray of coffee and each officer grabbed a cup; some to refresh themselves and others to make use of the warmth the coffee cups offered their freezing hands. The officers, Todd, Mary and Jan huddled like penguins, keeping close together, sharing their body warmth whilst they awaited news from Rocky and his handler.

"Sir." a shout came from the dog handler in the distance. "Sir, please come over here."

Todd broke away from the group and ran over to the rear of the allotments, where plots were uncultivated and largely deserted. He saw Rocky sitting in the middle of a plot of land, happily panting and looking pleased with himself.

"We've got something sir." The handler told Todd.

"Could it be a fox or anything else?" Todd asked him.

"No sir, the dog is trained to smell human flesh," he told Todd. "Whatever is under there, it comes from a human and a dead one at that."

Todd knew that they had found Tiffany. His gut instinct had let him right once again. He thanked the handler who threw Rocky a tennis ball which the dog caught in his mouth before returning to his handler's side.

Todd walked over to the officers who waited patiently in their huddle for the news he was bringing to them.

"Did you get the tent?" he asked Mary.

"Yes Guv. It's in Jan's van." Mary affirmed.

"Ok, get it, get the shovels, call the photographer again and make sure that fucking cameraman is nowhere near here when the body comes out." Todd pulled his mobile phone out of his pocket so he could ring the Borough Commander and let him know that very soon there would be one more murder statistic to add to their figures.

* * *

20:00 hours

It took two police officers about twenty minutes to fight their way through the wet ground. The rainwater had caused the mud to compact and it was like sticky clay as they dug down with their shovels. Eventually they uncovered a green tarpaulin and immediately stopped digging for fear of causing damage to what lay beneath it. Jan the SOCO took over along with the now present photographer, who documented every aspect of Jan's investigations; capturing each moment eternally on a digital file.

Jan used a brush to dust off the mud around the tarpaulin, no easy feat as the bush caused the wet mud to smear. She put anything she considered of significance into a plastic evidence bag; hairs, small bits of paper rubbish and sometimes almost invisible specks which she knew from experience may offer some evidence when scrutinised under a microscope.

Eventually, once Jan was happy she had scraped clean every possible scrap of evidence surrounding the tarpaulin, she gave the go ahead for two officers to retrieve the body length package from its hole. They took an end each then gently lifted the tightly rolled tarpaulin; it was so tightly ravelled that nothing escaped its embrace.

The tarp was laid on the floor and Todd watched from the side of the tented area whilst the officers slowly unravelled the green plastic. It was obvious that the contents of the tarpaulin were not featherweight; it took a real effort for the officers to turn it over and over until eventually a terrible smell began to emanate from the confines of the plastic. Dribbles of red liquid started to roll down from the creases of the tarp as it unravelled; Todd, Jan and the two officers all gave gasps of disgust as the smell of rotting flesh assaulted their noses. The liquid secretions became larger and darker in colour, browns and yellows mixed in with the reds and the last turn of the plastic revealed why. A rotten corpse, naked and torn was exposed to the air. Obviously female and a redhead, her body was a multitude of colours; purple being the main one where blood had settled and began to rot inside her. Todd knew this was Tiffany. The absence of formed breasts and the bare pubis showed this was a very young girl and the bright red hair screamed Tiffany at him. Looking closer, hand over mouth and nose in an attempt to block the smell, Todd could see the same raggedy bite marks in Tiffany's skin that had been present on Savannah's body.

One of the officers who had been unravelling the tarpaulin made a hasty exit from the tent and Todd could hear him evacuating the contents of his stomach outside the tent.

"Get away from the scene," he shouted out to the officer, although Todd knew that vomit would wait for no man.

"Oh the poor child," Jan said as she continued her constant picking of evidence from the tarpaulin and started moving towards Tiffany's body.

"Right, get the Coroner down here now." Todd said into the air knowing that Mary stood outside the tent. He walked out to where she stood. "We better tell the parents before them bastards go live." He said, gesturing to where Jogesh Singh was talking animatedly into the camera now pointed at him.

"Is it bad Guv?" Mary asked, having no desire to see for herself the devastation that lay inside the tent.

"It's the same person, I can tell you that much," Todd said, telling Mary about the bite marks, "I hope the bastard left some DNA because this time I'm going to nail that fucker."

"Well we'll know soon enough." Mary reassured him. "Jan will get those samples to the lab and we will know by the morning. Let's just hope he's on our database."

"Oh he's on it alright," Todd grimaced. "I know that Adrian Brown is responsible for doing this and I will be knocking on his door the minute the lab results confirm it."

Mary nodded in agreement and both she and Todd made their way to Todd's car in order to go and complete the unenviable task of letting Tiffany's parents know she would never be going home again.

Chapter 28

'Killing is not as easy as the innocent believe.'
*J.K. Rowling, Harry Potter and the Half Blood
Prince.*

24ᵗʰ May 2012
22:00 hours

Jocasta lolled on her sofa with one eye on the Ten
o'clock News and one eye shut. She was in a dozing
state but still slightly aware of what was being reported
on the television. When a picture of Twockford Rugby
Ground flashed up onto the screen, Jocasta immediately came to full attention, sitting up on the sofa and
turning up the volume on the television so she could
better hear the forthcoming report.

A serious presenter began to speak with the
tickertape headline below proclaiming, 'Body found
in Elisworth.' Footage was put up on the screen and
Jocasta immediately recognised the alleyway which led
to some allotments near Migdon Lane, the same allotments she realised, as where Savannah had been found.

Jocasta hoped beyond all hopes that the body
was that of an adult or a person who had met their
fate at the hands of an aggrieved loved one, but as

the newsreader told the story, Jocasta soon had those hopes crushed.

'The body of a young girl known as Tiffany Jones was discovered by police earlier in the evening.' The newscaster reported. 'Her parents had gone to the police earlier in the day to report Tiffany as missing; police quickly deployed search teams and a police sniffer dog discovered her remains buried on an allotment situated near to Twockford Rugby Ground.'

Remains; Jocasta flinched at the word as it was uttered by the reporter. The unfurling news report stuck a pin into Jocasta's heart with each word that came. She knew that Adrian had committed the crime that was being explained to the nation on the News. Once again Adrian had lied and manipulated her by making her believe that he had committed only one crime. When they had spoken in the kitchen and Adrian had screamed his crime at Jocasta, he had still been astute enough to withhold the knowledge he had of what he had done. Jocasta was absolutely devastated. She didn't know what to do with Adrian, she was now petrified that there could be other girls buried in those allotments awaiting discovery. Jocasta consoled herself that at least Adrian was safely tucked away in the prison she had created for him.

The next footage was like a lightning bolt to Jocasta's heart. She recognised the face of the handsome police officer who had visited her flat after Savannah had been killed. He spoke now, looking down the lens of the camera, his eyes were looking directly at her and boring a hole in her heart.

"We have today recovered the body of Tiffany Jones. She was an eleven year old girl who has been missing from her home for eight days. Tiffany has been taken to the Coroner's office and a full investigation is taking place."

The officer's eyes burned with emotion. Jocasta sat entranced by his piercing stare. "We will get the evidence we need and bring the perpetrator of this crime to justice. Thank you."

The officer began to turn away from the camera when one of the unseen reporters shouted out to him, "Have you a message for the killer Detective Inspector?" the question stopped him in his tracks and an obvious struggle fought its way across his facial features. He was obviously torn between his professionalism as a police officer and his emotional battle as a human being. He looked back at the camera and Jocasta felt the hairs rise on the back of her neck. Goose pimples prickled all over her body and blackness started to creep into her eyes. Her lips started to go numb and the last thing she heard before she fainted was, "I'm coming to get you."

* * *

Jocasta came around still lying on the sofa. The News was now finished and looking at the clock, she found that she had been unconscious for about ten minutes. Jocasta had never fainted before, she thought she must have stopped breathing whilst watching the news report; it was such a shocking revelation to her that her whole body had just shut down. Jocasta now knew that it would not be long until the officer on the television would come knocking on her door to take away her only son.

Jocasta was sickened by Adrian's actions. There was nothing inside her that could excuse what Adrian had done but she could not find the strength to hate him. Her love for Adrian was so overwhelmingly strong, he was her flesh and blood and she had borne the physical pain of bringing him into the world. The pain and heartache Adrian had given Savannah and her family and now Tiffany and *her* family, were devastating, but it was only something which Jocasta could imagine as she had not physically suffered that pain for herself. Whilst Jocasta had great sympathy for the girls and their families, her feelings for Adrian were greater and her emotions played a game of tug of war inside her head.

Jocasta's most burning issue was the fact Adrian would be taken away from her. He would be thrown into prison and the key would be well and truly thrown away. The sins of Adrian would surely follow him into the prison and he would be open to terrible abuse at the hands of either monsters or even the possibility of death at the hands of gangsters who considered themselves avenging angels.

Whilst Jocasta knew that Adrian probably deserved the fate which lay before him, she could not imagine her own life without Adrian there. Imagining her daily struggle knowing that Adrian was being tormented, would be the worst way for Jocasta to live, but there still remained the need for justice. Savannah and Tiffany's parents deserved closure and compensation for the children that had been so cruelly taken from them. Jocasta felt guilty that she still had her child when they spent every day mourning the loss of theirs.

Jocasta also wrestled with an overwhelming feeling of culpability. She had created Adrian; every organ inside him, every part of his skin, every finger, toe and nail on his body. She was his mother and had been responsible for both the nature and nurture of Adrian.

Any thought Adrian had and every deed he had done must surely have come from Jocasta. She felt ultimately responsible for everything Adrian had ever done as it was her blackened womb which had produced this wicked monster of a man.

Knowing that she could not live with the thought of Adrian being tormented in a prison cell and now accepting her part in the whole sordid situation; Jocasta made the decision to pay the price for Adrian's sins. Before she was able to do that, Jocasta needed to cleanse Adrian's soul and put her baby to rest.

She stood and slowly walked to Adrian's room, silently opening the door to the bedroom. Adrian remained prone in his bed, the Temazepam having had a sedating effect on him. Jocasta had already increased the dose so she could be sure he wouldn't awaken during the night and leave the flat.

She went over to the bed and stroked Adrian's

serene face. "I love you Adrian," She whispered. She then picked up a pillow which lay beside Adrian's head.

Jocasta put the pillow over Adrian's face then lay on top of it and held her son's face in a very tight embrace, putting her full weight over the area where she knew his face must be. Images flashed in Jocasta's mind.

Getting off the plane in Greece and feeling the warm sun on her skin.

Avram's smile as he introduced himself to her at the bar.

Her joy at the attention Avram gave her and the feeling of achievement and lust she felt when he took her virginity.

The sound of Adrian's heartbeat and the squirming body she saw on the ultrasound screen at the first scan.

Her looking at her belly as a large lump would appear where the foetus growing inside her stretched out an arm or leg and kicked her, playing an unheard tune inside her womb.

The sound of Adrian's cry as he was born and her fear when she realised there was something wrong with him.

An overwhelming heat of love enveloped Jocasta once again as she remembered looking at her new born baby and feeling the unbreakable bond between mother and child.

Walking away from the school, Adrian's screams of 'No mummy, don't leave me,' echoing in her ear.

Calling the headmaster a jumped up prick before removing Adrian from his first school.

Watching Adrian's smile as she pushed him on his bike and let go for the first time; his little legs pedalling furiously as he rode the bike, "Look mum, I'm doing it," He had shouted.

The utter despair when Adrian was found sick in his bed and her heart wrenching imagination of Adrian's premature death.

Hearing Adrian admit to touching Charmaine and her blind denial of the truth; choosing instead to buy him a new computer.

Adrian bucked underneath her; his body now suffering from the lack of oxygen. Adrian made no sound, the Temazepam making him unaware of his situation but an animal instinct for survival causing his body to fight against its killer. Had Jocasta still been thinking about Adrian as a child, she may have broken away but her thoughts had now jumped to the reasons she was committing the ultimate sin.

Adrian walking into their flat with wet legs from toe to knee.

Adrian convincing her to join the hunt for Savannah and then discovering he was the one who had found Savannah's body.

The sight of the single pair of knickers under Adrian's mattress and her first confirmation that Adrian had been responsible for Savannah's death.

Adrian screaming at her that it was all her fault; his twisted face close up in her own and the menace in his eyes when he called her a cunt.

The body beneath Jocasta stopped bucking and the smell of faeces filled the room. Jocasta held onto the pillow and her now dead son for a little longer; now holding the vision of Adrian as a new born baby in her mind.

She took the pillow away from Adrian's face and no longer saw an evil monster but a little boy, now absolved of his sins and at peace.

Jocasta picked Adrian's head up in her hands and placed it on her lap, shuffling underneath him so she could cuddle him properly. She knew it wouldn't be long before the police came to claim her and she wanted to spend as much time as possible with him before they were parted forever.

Jocasta then got up and left the room, returning with a bowl of hot soapy water. She hummed nursery rhymes as she washed Adrian down, changed him into a clean pair of pyjamas and laid him back on his now clean bed. "There Adrian, all clean," she whispered to his rapidly cooling corpse, "All better now," she said.

All images in Jocasta's mind were now pure, all focused on the beautiful smile of her son's face when he was a toddler, taking his first steps, his first words and she once again felt the pride a mother has for her children.

Tears streamed down Jocasta's face as she mourned her only son. She lay back onto the pillow and allowed the tears to flow freely down her chubby cheeks. The tears ran but Jocasta remained stoic; she had lost herself in the memories of Adrian. She was ready to pay the price for Adrian's sins by going to

Mother Be The Judge

prison for his murder. Jocasta hoped she would, in some way, have offered Savannah and Tiffany's parents the justice they deserved and they would be able to start the long road towards healing their emotional wounds. In Jocasta's mind her job as a mother was done.

Epilogue

'Motherhood, all love begins and ends there.'
Robert Browning.

25th *May 2012*

Detective Inspector Todd 'Todger' Turnbull had received the news at ten o'clock that morning. DNA evidence that had been collected by Jan at the scene of the crime in the form of a hair found on Tiffany's body, buried in the ragged bite mark on her stomach; confirmed that Adrian Brown was indeed guilty of committing the crimes against Tiffany.

Todd was not only pleased that his copper's instinct had been right all along, but he was pleased that there was a very real probability of getting the justice that the girls and their parents deserved.

When Todd heard the news over the telephone, he put the receiver down and hot footed it to the canteen, grabbing Detective Sergeant Mary Webb's 999 breakfast from under her nose and calling her to action.

They called the van to Adrian Brown's address so they could transport him back to the police station, then made their way in Todd's car to the Fern Bridge

Estate. Todd felt this was the most gratifying part of his job; his hard work, persistence and excellent investigative skills mixed with his natural ability to sniff out a wrong 'un, meant he was able to bring in the bad guys. He was filled with a kind of joy at the prospect of delivering Adrian Brown to justice.

* * *

Todd and Mary arrived at the front door of Adrian Brown's flat and knocked hard on the door, the two uniformed police officers waiting patiently behind them.

"Adrian Brown, it's the police." Todd shouted through the door. He had already phoned Big Value to check Adrian was not at work and had been informed Adrian had been sick for the last few days and had not been there.

"Adrian Brown," Todd shouted again, receiving no response.

"Get it open." Todd said to the waiting uniforms. One of them went to the police van and returned with a large red metal tube. It was known as the enforcer and was a very effective battering ram. Todd and Mary took a few steps back and watched as two swift knocks from the enforcer caused the fragile door to almost fly off its hinges. The uniformed officer moved to the side, allowing Todd and Mary to enter the flat.

Todd walked slowly around the flat; he entered

the kitchen followed by Mary, it was empty except for the remains of chocolate wrappers strewn across the kitchen table and a packet of tablets propped up near the sink. Todd picked up the packet and read the prescription for Temazepam in the name of Georgina Perkins, which was written across the front. He checked inside, fearing it may be empty but found there were only eight missing from the bubble pack inside.

Todd moved into the front room, again finding it empty. Finally he moved to the unopened door at the end of the hallway.

Todd opened the door to the bedroom and walked in to see two figures lying, apparently asleep in the single bed.

Closer inspection revealed to Todd that the male lying in the bed was dead, his skin was very white and purple blotches were present on his ears and the parts of the head which were touching the bed.

The rise and fall of the females' chest and her open eyes which silently watched Todd's progress across the room, told him that Jocasta Brown was very much alive.

"I killed him." Jocasta told Todd. "He can't hurt any more girls."

Todd sighed. He was filled with pity for the woman that lay in bed cradling her son. He now had to arrest her for the murder of Adrian Brown and take away her liberty. He couldn't decide if he was angry at Jocasta for robbing both him and the girls' parents of the chance to seek justice, or whether he was grateful

Mother Be The Judge

that she had meted out the most desirable punishment for such an evil deed *and* had made the ultimate sacrifice in the quest for that justice.

"Jocasta Brown, I'm arresting you for the murder of Adrian Brown. You do not have to say anything, but it may harm your defence if you do not mention when questioned something which you later rely on in court. Anything you do say may be given in evidence."

Mary stepped forward and took Jocasta's hands away from Adrian; she gently helped Jocasta to her feet and put handcuffs on her, then began to lead her away from the bed.

"I had to do it." Jocasta looked back at Adrian.

"I had to do it." She turned and looked at Mary Webb.

"I had to do it." She looked to Todd.

"I know." Todd said sighing. "I know." He took Jocasta from Mary's hands and led her to the waiting police van.

Another murder solved. Another killer caught. Another statistic on a police bar chart. Todd's belly rumbled and his mind turned to the thoughts of a big fat breakfast as he walked back with Mary to his car, job done, crime solved, moving on.

Printed in Great Britain
by Amazon.co.uk, Ltd.,
Marston Gate.